A-M-O-R

and other stories

by **SCOTT RICHMOND**

Copyright ©2019
Scott Richmond

Library of Congress
Cataloguing-in-Publication Data

Published by
4Rivers Press

Richmond, Scott.
A-M-O-R
Scott Richmond.
–1st ed.

ISBN: 978-0-9633067-7-7

Design:
Eric Hillerns

Copy Editing:
Karen Brattain

Set in Paperback and
Clarendon.

For Gillian, sister
and first friend

Also by
Scott Richmond

The Pocket Gillie

*Fishing in Oregon's
Deschutes River*
(First Edition)

*Fishing in Oregon's
Cascade Lakes*

*Fishing in Oregon's
Endless Season*

*Fishing in Oregon's
Best Fly Waters*

*River Journal: Crane
Prairie Reservoir*

*River Journal:
Rogue River*

*Fishing Oregon's
Deschutes River*
(Second Edition)

River in the Sun

Contents

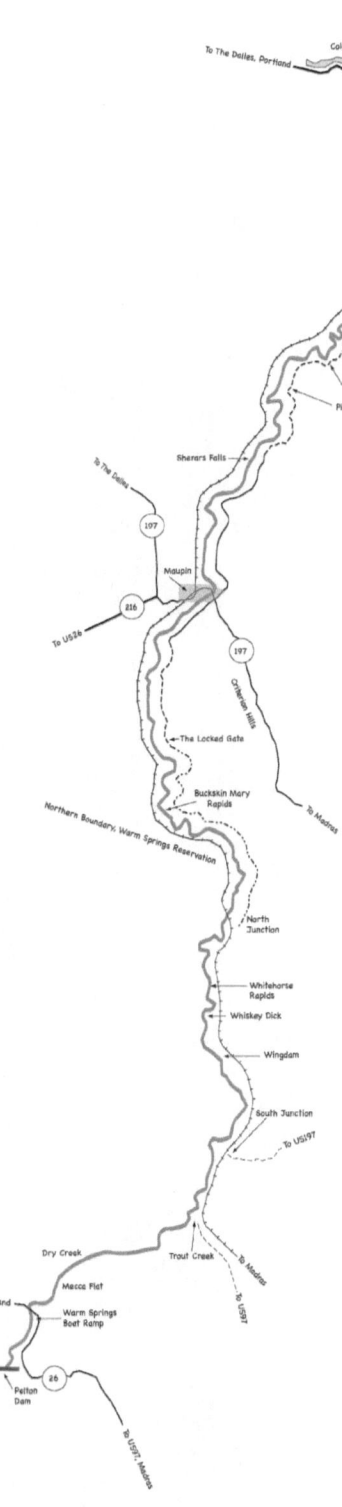

A-M-O-R

and other stories

by **SCOTT RICHMOND**

Judd

April 16: Deschutes River at Trout Creek

THERE WAS A TIME WHEN Judd Boone's Stetson was crisp, clean, and light brown. But that was a long time ago, before years of guiding fly anglers on the Deschutes River warped the brim, scuffed the crown, and sun-blasted the color to an indistinct tan punctuated by sweat stains.

This morning, Judd wore his hat square and tipped forward, as was his habit when angry. He looked at his watch for the third time in five minutes and shook his head. "Where is that damn kid?" he said.

He spoke these words aloud, although no one was at the Trout Creek boat ramp to hear him. That was, in fact, the problem: no one was there to hear him. Casey Williams was half an hour late. And he'd told Judd he'd be there early.

The two of them were supposed to drift the Deschutes River between Trout Creek and Maupin, each in his own boat, and check out campsites and fishing runs to see how they'd fared over the winter. Judd called it First Float, and it had to be done before the year's first clients showed up. It was a two-boat, two-person job, and this was the day to do it. "Damn kid!" he said again.

Judd walked around his boat one more time, rattling the oars, fiddling with the anchor, and fuming about Casey. What was he going to do with him? The kid had flaked out! Again! Next time he saw him … well, it would be the *last* time he saw him. Yeah, the very last time. Write him his final paycheck then boot his sorry butt out on the street. Casey could work for somebody else. As if anyone else would take on such an immature, unreliable, won't grow up, worthless …

Judd sighed and pushed his Stetson to the back of his head, as was his habit when trying to think something through. He recalled the time twelve years ago when Casey was a troubled, at-risk seventeen-year-old and Judd had stepped in and given the kid the mentoring he needed. Yes, there had been plenty of rough patches, but Casey eventually became a good fishing guide and a responsible young man—enough so that Judd now called him his head fishing guide, although most of the season Casey was the *only* guide other than Judd.

Perhaps Casey had a good excuse for being late. Maybe his truck had broken down. Or there had been an accident. Casey's pickup might be upside down in a ditch. Casey might be injured. Worse. The highway coming over Mt. Hood often iced up at this time of year. But Casey was a good driver and knew how to deal with it. But those other yahoos on the road …

Judd had to admit—to himself, never to Casey, of course—that he thought of Casey almost like a son. An occasionally prodigal, often frustrating sort of son, but a son nonetheless.

He took two deep breaths and wiped his brow, even though he wasn't hot. If he didn't immediately start down the river, he reasoned, there wouldn't be enough time to finish before dark. If Casey was delayed for some reason, he'd get to the boat ramp and figure that Judd had started out; then he'd row hard and catch up. If Casey had

had an accident—God forbid—there was nothing Judd could do about it. And if Casey had just plain screwed up? Well, Judd would deal with it later.

One thing was clear: he couldn't hang around the boat ramp fussing about things that were beyond his control. He adjusted his Stetson to its normal position, slid his driftboat into the river, and started downstream.

Two miles on, just below Trout Creek Rapids, he anchored and went ashore. He examined the campsites, checked the outhouse, and glanced at the fishing spots to see if they had changed over the winter. Then he got back in his boat and continued downriver.

Now that he'd started out, Judd calmed down. He'd done this trip in a day many times in his career, mostly for sightseers. At fifty-eight years old, he was not as young as he used to be, but he could still do this. And he had to admit that he enjoyed floating the river solo, especially in the spring. The grass was greening up; the willows and alders were covered with bright buds and new leaves. Now and then he heard the sharp call of an osprey or the rattle of a kingfisher. In smooth stretches he could rest the oars and admire the canyon walls rising nearly a thousand feet above him. This was his office, his place of work, and he loved it.

More than thirty years ago, Judd's ailing father had handed him the reins of the very modest OK Cafe and Resort in Maupin. In addition to running the old family business, Judd had started the Rainbow Anglers Guide Service, or RAGS as Judd referred to it—usually ironically. He'd left a good job and a promising career to take care of fly anglers and river rafters. He might make less money than most of his clients, but he never regretted his decision. His wife, Susan, managed the cafe and its six cabins while Judd was on the river; he knew she was as content as he.

ONE BY ONE, JUDD CHECKED out the campsites, gave prime

fishing spots the once-over, and surveyed the state of the river. By the
time the sun kissed the canyon's western rimrock, he'd covered
thirty-two miles of river and twenty-six campsites. He'd not done as
thorough a job as he would have liked—sometimes he'd just done a
quick float-by, a mere lick-and-a-promise—but it would be sufficient.
All the major rapids were behind him now, and it was only eight miles
to the takeout ramp; he'd be there a little after dark. He looked
forward to a hot meal and a soft bed.

As he passed a cluster of cabins on a private road, he saw
someone on the riverbank waving him over. Judd thought the man
might be in trouble, so he rowed toward him. Fifty feet out, he
realized it was Merv Andreeson. Judd reflexively closed his eyes and
tightened his jaw. *This will be a waste of time*, he thought, and tugged
his Stetson square and low.

Judd had known Merv for many years, but he didn't like being
around him anymore. *Nobody* liked being around Merv anymore. The
man had aged into anger and self-pity and sometimes gave long
political rants devoid of logic and consistency. Merv had inherited a
cabin from his father, and he often stayed there to fish and drink—
but lately, mostly to drink.

"Buddy is lost!" Merv said as Judd dropped his anchor. Buddy,
a mid-sized dog of obscure ancestry, was Merv's only companion
since his wife left him. "I can't find him anywhere!"

"Ah, that's too bad," Judd said, bending over to pull up his
anchor and be on his way. "Well, I'll keep an eye out for him."

"He might be in trouble!" Merv said. "It's getting dark, and I
don't want the coyotes to get him."

Judd thought Buddy might be better off taking his chances with
the coyotes rather than staying with Merv, but he said, "Where have
you looked?"

Merv waved an arm upstream. "A mile above the house. And
half a mile below." He shook his head. "No sign of him. I called and
called. He didn't bark or anything."

"They say that if you put your shirt or jacket on the ground and walk away, you'll find the dog lying on it a couple of hours later. Why don't you try that?"

"In a couple of hours Buddy could be some coyote's dinner." Merv dropped his head, eyes closed. "Oh, God! What will I do without him? He's my best friend!"

More like only *friend,* Judd thought, and that made him feel sorry for Merv. He pushed his Stetson to the back of his head. "I don't know what to tell you, Merv." He put on a cheery face. "Buddy's a smart dog. He'll find his way home. You'll see." He pulled up the anchor and reached for his oars. "And I'll keep my eyes peeled as I go down the river."

"Does that coat trick really work? Have you tried it?"

Judd shipped his oars and dropped the anchor. Apparently a quick getaway was not in the cards. "Umm. No, I haven't tried it myself. But I know someone who did." He couldn't remember if it had worked or not.

Merv shook his head. "I don't know. I just don't know." There was more head shaking. "Judd—"

"How's the old cabin doing? Roof holding up?" Judd knew what was coming next and wanted to change the subject.

"Roof's okay," Merv said. "Mary made me fix it last year. Before she left me." Merv looked like he was going to cry. "God, why did she leave me? I've got to get Buddy back. I'm so lonely. I wish Mary hadn't left. Why did she go?"

"Hard to say about these things." *Perhaps being mean and angry when you're drunk—and being drunk a lot of the time—had something to do with it.* "Women can be a mystery, can't they."

"Judd ... I can't go on like this. I need to stop drinking. Next week I'm starting again with AA. Take another run at it."

"Good for you, Merv. I wish you all the luck in the world. Let me know if I can help." He reached for the anchor line.

"It would be easier for me if I had Buddy for company. Will you help me find Buddy?"

"Well … well I …" Judd looked everywhere but at Merv. "I'd like to, but …" *Ah crap.* "Okay." *Why can't I just keep my damn yap shut!* "Sure. I'll help you look."

"Thanks! You're a real friend!"

No, I'm an idiot who doesn't know when to mind his own business. "Any time. Glad to help." After getting out of his boat, he took a whistle from his pocket and handed it to Merv. "Take this. If you find the dog, let me know. And if I find him, I'll let you know." He jangled a whistle that hung on his jacket. "I keep these around to herd my fishing clients. We'll meet at the boat. In any case, we meet in one hour, dog or no dog. I'm going to be running this river by Braille as it is." They parted, with Merv heading upstream and Judd walking downriver.

Fact was, Judd had little expectation of success. Either the dog would wander home on his own, or someone else would find him. Or the coyotes had already gotten him. Or he'd been hit by a train, or fallen into the river and drowned, or gotten snakebit and died. Or just run away from Merv—why not? Everyone else had left him.

But Merv needed something to cling to, some kind of companionship, something to get him from one day to the next. And who knew? Maybe Merv would get his act together and sober up. And having a dog could prove to be the key.

Or not. It's devilish hard to know if you're really helping someone or just enabling them to perpetuate their bad behavior.

Then Judd thought about Casey, whom he had put out of mind for most of the day. Casey hadn't showed up at the boat ramp on time, so maybe his old unreliable, irresponsible nature had reasserted itself.

Judd wondered: how could you know when to help someone and when to mind your own business? Sometimes you try to help and only make things worse. It was a lot easier to tell his fishing clients which fly to tie on. God forbid they should ask him what to do with their lives.

Twilight deepened in the canyon, so Judd pulled a small flashlight from his jacket and aimed it at the ground. It had rained the night before, leaving the ground damp in places, and he occasionally saw Merv's footprints from his earlier search for Buddy. He even found the place where Merv had turned around and headed back upstream. Judd kept walking. A couple of hundred yards farther, he saw what he least expected: a paw print. He stooped and examined the print. Coyote or domestic dog? Hard to say. But the print was fresh and about the right size for Buddy.

Not far away, a coyote let out a piercing *yip-yip-yip-yiiiip*. Judd quickened his pace, following the tracks as best he could. He spotted a dark mass ahead, probably a pile of debris that had washed up in the high flows of winter. As he neared it, a pair of eyes reflected brightly in the flashlight's beam. Judd walked on and found Buddy; his right front leg was caught in a tangle of rusty barbed wire.

Judd knelt and rubbed the dog's head. Buddy licked his hand, trembling. "You're a smart cookie," Judd said to the dog as he carefully extricated his leg from the wire. "You didn't struggle. That would have made it worse. And you knew that if you barked, the coyotes would have heard you." He freed the dog then pulled out his whistle.

IT HAD BEEN DARK FOR TWO HOURS by the time Judd reached the Harpham Flat boat ramp. He was knackered, and he felt a headache coming on—too much work, too much stress, too much thinking about whether he'd done the right thing or not.

Over the last few miles, he'd decided that helping Merv was pointless; Merv was never going to get sober. He should have freed Buddy and quietly let him go. All he'd done was prolong the poor dog's miserable life with Merv. And most of all, he'd probably failed with Casey. From now on, he decided, Judd Boone was going to mind his own goddam business. The world was going to have to get along without his advice and interference.

When he drove into Maupin, Judd stared in amazement. There were bright lights and a crowd of people milling around the Drift Inn. Or what was left of the Drift Inn. The old hotel had stood three doors down from the OK Cafe for almost a hundred years. But now it was a pile of charred, smoldering wood. In the lights, Judd could see a county sheriff's car and a fire truck. Judd parked in the OK's lot and stepped from his pickup, wondering.

His wife Susan charged out of the cafe, the screen door banging behind her. "It's okay, Judd!" Susan said as she ran up to him. "Everyone's fine. Well, Casey and Old Ernie are in the hospital, and Ernie's not in great shape. But Casey's going to be fine. Don't worry."

"Casey?" Judd said. "What—"

"He's going to be fine. They've got him in for observation. Smoke inhalation."

"Smoke ... inhalation?"

"He saw the fire as he drove down the road. About quarter to six."

"Quarter to six?" At that rate Casey would have been to Trout Creek half an hour early. *Huh! What a kid!*

Susan nodded. "The smoke was coming from under the eaves, and the fire was spreading when he got there. Then he saw Old Ernie's car in the parking lot. He broke in the door of the Drift Inn and crawled along the floor until he saw Ernie, then pulled him out. They think a beam fell on him. Hit him on the head, they think."

"Fell on Casey?" Judd felt like the world was spinning around him.

"No. On Ernie. He was unconscious when Casey pulled him out. Not from the smoke, though. From being hit on the head. They think he'll recover but don't really know. But if Casey hadn't dragged him out, Ernie would have died for sure."

Judd put a hand on his truck to steady himself. "Casey? My head guide? Ran into a burning building? Risked his life to drag out that old geezer?" He shook his head. "I'll be go-to-hell."

"Casey was real worried that you wouldn't understand why he wasn't at Trout Creek. He was still talking about it when they loaded him into the ambulance." She put her hand on Judd's shoulder. "Don't worry. He'll be fine."

"No, no. I'm not worried." He took a breath and shook his head for the twentieth time. "So Casey ran into a burning building."

"That's the size of it. Say, why are you so late? I've been fixing food for the firemen and the sheriff, so I … well, I forgot about you until half an hour ago. Then I was pretty worried." Susan took his hand in her own. "What made you so late?"

"Oh, nothing. It took extra time because I was alone. And I ran into Merv Andreeson. His dog Buddy—remember Buddy, that brindled mutt?—he was lost, and I helped look. We found him, too."

"That's good."

"I guess." Judd surveyed the smoking ruins of the Drift Inn. "So Casey's a hero. Well, it's been quite a day in Hoppin' Maupin."

"Judd," Susan said quietly, "don't forget who else is a hero."

"Huh?"

"Sure, Casey saved Ernie. But who saved Casey? You did. If you hadn't helped Casey, who would have been there for Ernie?" She squeezed his hand. "It's ripples in the pond, you know."

"That is one murky pond," Judd said, rolling his eyes.

"Seems to be, sometimes." Susan chewed her lip, then asked, "How is Merv doing? I see Mary now and then in The Dalles. She says his drinking is worse than ever. She's worried about him."

"Merv said he's going to take another run at AA."

"Maybe it will work this time."

"Yeah, you never know." Judd pushed his Stetson to the back of his head. "Maybe this will be the time that Merv sticks with it." He smiled. "At least he's got a dog to keep him company."

7 X

May 7: Deschutes River, South Junction

WHEN NICK ARRIVED AT THE DESCHUTES a little after dawn, the river was high and turbid—the color of the double-shot latte he'd consumed on the way up from Portland. Apparently an intense thunderstorm had rolled through the canyon last night. He cursed his luck. There would be no fly fishing here today.

Nick considered his options. He could forget about fishing and return to Portland; but then he'd feel obligated to go into the office, and he needed a break from his job and the stress that went with it. Or he could head for the Metolius, a Deschutes tributary that wouldn't be affected by the storm. But he hadn't fished the Metolius for six years—had avoided it like toxic waste, in fact.

Two options, neither of them attractive. He paced back and forth, thinking it over, but he knew he was just procrastinating, giving his mind time to adjust to a change of plan. Five minutes later he started for the Metolius.

His aversion to the Metolius had nothing to do with the river itself, which many people consider postcard-perfect. The Metolius originates near Black Butte, a volcanic cone that rises above the surrounding forests like a king on his throne. The river issues from lava rock at its base—mature and full-flowing at birth. The pure water has a blue-green clarity like ancient crystal. A parklike forest of old-growth ponderosa pines surrounds the river.

Fishing there is often sublime, but never easy. The clear waters delude a casual angler into thinking the river is easily comprehended, but there are sudden drops, hidden springs, and unseen channels. They sculpt a current whose twists and force are difficult to anticipate.

Six years ago, Nick fished the Metolius often. Then he shunned it and frequented other streams. He made excuses: too far to drive, fishing too demanding, didn't have the right flies.

But when he was honest with himself, he knew there was only one reason he avoided the Metolius: it was Ethan McVey's favorite river.

SIX YEARS AGO, ETHAN MCVEY became the manager of the computer sales group in which Nick worked. At the time, Nick was thirty-two years old, and Ethan was forty-seven.

Nick liked Ethan at once. He was what sales people call a *gray eminence*, a mature man with a confident bearing that helps establish a relationship of trust and respect with a customer.

Although Nick was a natural achiever and could easily empathize with people—the raw ingredients of a successful sales career—he needed polishing. Ethan taught him the finer points, such as, "When you take a prospect to lunch, never discuss business until he's ordered his meal. He can't make a business decision until he's chosen his food." Another time he told Nick, "Always point with an instrument of quality. And your finger isn't it. Carry an expensive pen, and use it for a pointer."

Ethan had an interest in fly fishing, a hobby he'd picked up two years before—just after his bypass surgery. When he learned that Nick had been fly fishing since his teens, Ethan suggested they go to the Metolius. Ethan had heard good things about the river and wanted to experience its beauty and grace firsthand. He and Nick made their first trip together in late May.

It was sunny when they arrived, but at that high elevation, the air was still crisp. They walked to the river past tall ponderosa pines, their orange-brown trunks rising forty feet or more before the first limbs stretched out. Long three-fingered needles rustled soft and deep in the wind and cast a shimmering mosaic of shadows on the pine-scented forest floor.

Trout occasionally dimpled the river as they sipped large, olive-bodied insects from the water's surface. Nick collected one of the insects. "Green drakes!" he said, holding one out for Ethan. *"Drunella grandis"* he added, giving the Latin name.

Ethan looked at it closely. "It's some kind of mayfly?"

Nick had forgotten that he knew far more about fly fishing than Ethan. He pointed out the chief features of the insect. Then Ethan got out his fly box and stood uncomfortably while Nick peered at its contents. Ethan's flies were few; most were the glittery type bought by novice fly fishers who don't understand what they're trying to imitate. Nick offered Ethan a few flies from his own box.

Ethan walked downstream about a hundred feet and started casting. Nick quickly realized that Ethan was a poor caster. He waded to Ethan and gave a mini casting lesson, then showed him how to mend line so the fly would float naturally. "Why don't you go downstream and work that flat water," Nick suggested, pointing out a stretch that offered easy casting and simple currents.

Ethan pointed to where a trout had just risen near them. "There are more fish here," he said.

"Trust me," Nick said. "You'll find the fishing better down there."

Ethan took a few more casts where he stood, then moved grudgingly to the spot Nick had pointed out. He soon had a trout on the end of his line, and his good spirits returned. By the time they broke for lunch, Ethan was full of stories. He had an infectious sense of humor; he could have told the story in Chinese, and you'd have laughed just because he laughed.

Some of his stories were about wild dates. Ethan was tall and lean, and his graying temples gave him a distinguished look. He was currently single, and women found him attractive. Although Nick was happily married, he took vicarious pleasure in Ethan's tales.

Nick was acquainted with one of the women Ethan had dated, a high-tech sales rep named Teresa Gordon. She and Nick had cooled their heels in the same corporate lobbies, and through small talk he knew that she and Ethan had gone out together.

"Didn't you date Teresa Gordon?" Nick asked Ethan.

Ethan's face clouded over. "Yeah. We were together about a year." He scowled. "She really torqued me off, and we broke up."

EVERY FEW WEEKS THROUGH the rest of the summer, Nick and Ethan trekked to the Metolius. Thanks to Nick's quiet suggestions, Ethan's casting had improved, and he could now lay out forty feet of line, straight and accurate.

However, he couldn't get the hang of mending. Mending is a critical skill because the fly line often lies across bands of current that move at different speeds. If the angler makes no adjustments, the fly will drag, rather than drift naturally with the river. So a good angler will mend—adjust how his line lies on the water—to delay or minimize drag. Mending needs to be done subtly, or very few trout will rise to the fly. Ethan never got it. Still, if he'd simply changed his position—cast from a different place—he could have improved his odds of hooking a fish. But he wouldn't do that either.

Nick suggested they try some other rivers. He couldn't tell Ethan why, of course. How do you tell your boss he's not very good? But Ethan insisted on going to the Metolius. "It's so beautiful there!" he'd say. But Ethan's inability to mend, combined with his unwilling- ness to change his standpoint, meant that he seldom reaped what the river offered and was frequently frustrated and angry.

The drives to the river always started well enough, with Ethan eagerly anticipating a day of fly fishing. But sometimes the ride home would be unpleasant. Nick would drive while Ethan looked sullenly out the window at the dark woods. Sometimes he'd talk about people he didn't like, people who—in his view—had treated him badly. Once he said, "You know, I really hate my father. The older I get, the more I hate that bastard." Nick knew that Ethan's father had died fifteen years ago.

Nick told that him that people weren't as bad as he thought, but Ethan would have none of it. Nick pushed the point as hard as he dared but knew when to back off. After all, Ethan was his boss. They might have a special relationship because of the fly fishing trips— and because Nick was the top sales rep in the group—but Nick knew there where times when he needed to keep his mouth shut.

THAT FALL THEY DROVE UP to the Metolius for the October caddis hatch. They'd had a tough quarter, sales-wise, and were both feeling stressed from work. Nick hoped the fishing trip would help them both relax.

The river was crowded, so they fished together about a hundred feet apart. Ethan was struggling with his casting again—a regression that frustrated Nick. Perhaps the work stress was making Ethan's muscles tight. "Remember to stop your backcast at one o'clock!" he called up to Ethan. "Closer to twelve, really. Cast with your arm, not your wrist."

Ethan continued to cast as before, breaking his wrist and bringing the rod too far back.

"For God's sake, Ethan," Nick muttered to himself. He went up to Ethan to show him what to do.

Ethan was red-faced when Nick reached him. "I can cast fine," he said. "Shut up and go back to your fishing."

Nick spoke gently and, he thought, patiently. "Just pretend there's a sheet of plywood behind you, and that you can't hit it with your rod."

As Nick walked back to his fishing spot, he could feel Ethan glaring at his back. A few casts later, he looked back at Ethan. His casting was better, but on every drift his fly would drag unnaturally. "Mend, Ethan!" Nick yelled at him. Two anglers upstream from them were looking their way. One made a quiet comment to the other, who laughed.

Nick walked briskly back to Ethan. "Look," he said softly, "the current is tricky here. You have to throw in a mend to keep your fly from dragging. See where it's moving fast?" Nick pointed with his rod to the water near them. "Out where the fish are, it's slower. You've got to mend line upstream in the fast water. Otherwise your fly vectors across …"

"*Vector?*" Ethan said. "Is that one of those college words?"

"I'm just talking about speed and direction," Nick said. "Your fly is going to—"

"Since you're such a smart ass, you catch these fish. I'm going upstream."

Nick looked at his retreating back, then made a perfect cast, followed by a perfect mend into the water Ethan had just left. His fly drifted about three feet before a trout rose and took it. "Fish on!" he yelled, feeling triumphant. The trout ran upstream and jumped opposite Ethan. "Nice fish!" Nick said loudly. Ethan looked the other way and kept walking.

Nick rolled his eyes and shook his head as Ethan left the river. After releasing the trout, he wondered what to do next. Follow Ethan? No—they needed a cooling-off period. The work stress was eating away at both of them, he figured. For his part, Nick knew he wouldn't normally have pushed things like he had. He needed some time to himself so he could regain his equilibrium. Ethan probably felt the same way.

He decided to go upstream and hiked the riverside trail, scanning the water for rises. Soon he saw a dimple near the bank. Rings of water spread out with a size and momentum that said "big trout." He looked closely and was rewarded with another rise. The trout was not taking the big October caddis, but little blue-winged olives, a small mayfly. On the river, he spied an occasional newly hatched blue-wing drifting on the current then lifting off as its wings dried. Bugs that drifted near the riverbank, though, were sipped by the trout before they could take to the air.

Nick moved cautiously to the river and crouched about forty feet below the rises. The fish was in two feet of water with a ledge to its left, so it had a quick exit. A small bankside willow was just upstream and shaded the water.

His first cast was too short. A second cast hit the willow then dropped onto the water. He tensed as the fly drifted toward the trout. There was no rise. After the fly passed, the fish rose to take a natural insect.

Nick sighed. The current was twisted here because of the way it flowed over the ledge, and it was midday. His 6X leader was probably too thick and stiff. Fly anglers refer to leaders by their diameter, or "X" size—how many thousandths of an inch less than eleven-thousandths—so 6X is five-thousandths of an inch, very thin indeed. Nick clipped back some of the 6X and tied on three feet of 7X, an even thinner material and the most delicate and fragile leader he carried;

just a little too much strain will separate fly from leader. He didn't like to use 7X, but sometimes there's no choice.

He waited until the trout reached a steady feeding rhythm, then timed his cast to match it. The fly drifted slowly to the fish's lie. A nose tipped up, pushing rings of water, and his fly disappeared. He had a brief glimpse of an arching dark green back and yellow-green tail. It was a good fish—not a trophy but probably eighteen inches. On 7X, though, any fish is big.

After five minutes of cautious play, he had the trout close and lifted his rod high. He reached out, pulling the fish to his hand. The trout saw his outstretched hand and pulled away. Nick gave no slack but tried to force the trout to him.

The tippet snapped, and the trout was gone.

HE FISHED UNSUCCESSFULLY for another hour before heading to the car. Ethan would have simmered down, he figured, and Nick would act apologetic and smooth things over. But when he reached the car, a piece of yellow paper was under the wiper blade. "Will get home on my own," the note read. There was no signature, but the handwriting was Ethan's.

Nick drove up the road looking for him. About two miles from the parking lot he spotted Ethan, doggedly walking alongside the road in his waders and vest, sweaty-faced and with his rod in his right hand.

Nick rolled down the window. "Hop in," he said, trying to sound normal. Ethan kept walking and didn't answer. Nick matched the pace of the car to Ethan's walk. "Come on," he said. "Get in. Let's get something to eat then go home."

"I'll get back on my own," Ethan answered without looking Nick's way.

"You're going to walk 150 miles like that? You'll wear holes in your waders." Nick thought if he cajoled a little—tried a little humor—Ethan would come around.

"Fuck you." Ethan said. And that was all he said. Nick followed him a quarter mile and was ignored the whole way. Finally, he drove to the road junction at Camp Sherman. Ethan would probably stop at the store and be tired enough to come with him.

Half an hour later Ethan puffed up to the store, looked past Nick, and asked if he could use the phone. Nick couldn't hear his call, but after hanging up, Ethan came over and said, "I got a ride. Push off."

The next day at work, Nick was passing the coffee station. Bob Armstrong, the service supervisor, was pouring himself a cup. "Ethan called me yesterday," he said to Nick. "He had me pick him up at Camp Sherman on the Metolius. He said he had car trouble. I owed him because he saved my butt during that network fiasco out at Transcept." Bob ripped open a package of creamer and poured it into his coffee. "It was a hell of a long drive, so I figure I don't owe him any more." He stirred the coffee. "How come he didn't call you? I thought you guys went up there all the time."

Nick shrugged and walked off.

NICK KEPT TO HIMSELF FOR a few days and avoided Ethan. At the end of the next week, Ethan called a staff meeting. Each sales rep in the group presented a forecast for the next quarter and talked about how to achieve it. Nick was first because he had the highest sales in the group and the most important accounts. After his presentation, Ethan tore into him like a pit bull. He ridiculed Nick's strategies and said his forecasts were fantasies.

Nick didn't fight it. What would have been the point? Everybody else looked frightened and embarrassed, probably thinking Ethan would rip them apart, too. He didn't.

A few days later, Nick ran into Teresa Gordon, Ethan's former girlfriend, in the lobby of a mutual customer. "Would you talk to me about Ethan McVey?" he asked. "I'm having a little trouble getting along with him."

"Who isn't?" she said, and shook her head. "Yeah, let's talk. Can we go outside? I'm dying for a smoke." Nick pushed open the glass door, and they walked to the visitors' lot. Teresa was in her early thirties, thin and angular-faced, but she had large, penetrating eyes and long, jet-black hair. She was appealing, in a high-strung kind of way. She lit a cigarette and smoked nervously while Nick told her how Ethan was acting. After he'd talked a few minutes, she tipped her head back, blew out a cloud of smoke, and interrupted him. "Look," she said. "Forget him. This is typical Ethan stuff. There's nothing you can do."

"But it's so childish, so petty."

"Yup, we're talking about the same guy. Jekyll and Hyde himself. Themselves. Whatever. Ethan is great at establishing relationships, but he wrecks every one of them. Sooner or later you walk on his pride, and he can't forgive that." She tapped some ash off the cigarette. "Or anything else."

"I thought he and I got along pretty well," Nick said. "We went fly fishing on the Metolius, and—"

"Look," Teresa said, "he was good after his bypass surgery. I even thought of getting back together with him. When he's good, he's really good. But when he's bad ..." She shook her head. "He was on the upswing, and that's when he got promoted to head your unit. Now I think you're seeing the old Ethan, the real Ethan."

"Maybe," Nick said grudgingly. "It's like he's grown ... I don't know ... more intolerant, less patient."

"That's the real Ethan," Teresa said. "You nick him, and he gets a big scar and spends the rest of his life looking at it and hating your guts for giving it to him. He can only love for a while, but he hates forever." She took a long pull on her cigarette then threw it, half-smoked, onto the asphalt and ground it out with her shoe. "Forget him," she said. "Like everyone else he's screwed over."

Still, Nick thought it was worth a try. Their common interest in fly fishing might be a foundation on which to rebuild friendship. He went to Ethan's office and sat in the chair beside his desk making small talk. Ethan's answers were short, and he looked annoyed. Nick pressed ahead anyway. "How about some fly fishing on the Metolius?" he said, exuding more enthusiasm than he felt. "Let's take a day off and go up there."

"I'm going next week," Ethan said. "Alone." He turned back to the papers he was working on. Nick waited another minute, but Ethan never looked up.

A month later there was an opening for a new sales manager in another group. It would be a good career step for Nick, and he wouldn't have to work for Ethan anymore. He applied for the position but couldn't even get an interview. "I'm sorry," the HR manager said, "but your last job review wasn't good, and we can't even consider you for the position." She showed Nick the paperwork. Nick's sales were tops in his group, yet Ethan rated him as "below average" and "needs improvement." The review was dated two weeks earlier.

"Mr. McVey didn't show this to you?" the HR manager asked with raised eyebrows. "Supervisors are supposed to go over these with their subordinates." She pushed the job review to him. He picked it up and stalked out.

Nick raged into Ethan's office, rattling the review. "You didn't even have the guts to show this to me!" he yelled.

"I was just trying to be fair and honest," Ethan said, palms upraised like he actually believed it.

Nick threw the paperwork on Ethan's desk and left.

He updated his resume and sent it around. Two months later he was hired to open the Portland sales office for a hot new company. He never went to the Metolius for the October caddis or any other hatch. The river reminded him of Ethan McVey, and every time he thought of Ethan McVey, he got tense and angry.

NICK ARRIVED AT THE METOLIUS a bit after 9:00 and parked near Wizard Falls. After putting on his chest waders and stringing his fly rod, he walked across the wooden bridge and headed upstream along the trail.

He walked head down, blind to the tall majestic pines and spreading cedars, oblivious to the clear and sparkling river. He decided it was a mistake to come to the Metolius today. Everything reminded him of that trip six years ago. He should have gone straight home after seeing the Deschutes was muddied-out. Ethan McVey— what a bastard! Served him right that his career went into a death spiral just as Nick's blossomed. It's true: success is the best revenge.

But after half a mile of angry, stiff-legged walking beside the crystalline river, Nick admitted that some of his professional success was due to Ethan. Every time he took out his expensive pen and used it to point out some feature of a sales contract, every time he took a client to lunch and waited to discuss business until his guest had ordered a meal, Nick was reminded of Ethan. He'd tried to push those thoughts aside, but they came anyway.

Even now, as he walked the trail by the Metolius, he occasionally found himself thinking of the good times he'd shared with Ethan. He almost expected to see him sitting on a log, ready to tell a funny story. But that wouldn't happen; Ethan had died of heart failure two years before, unreconciled with his family or his former friends.

Another half mile brought Nick to the place he'd hooked and lost a nice fish on his last trip with Ethan. As before, a trout was rising to an occasional blue-winged olive mayfly. An experienced angler would not consider this a coincidence: the features of current and overhead cover made this a good lie for a trout. Unless something changed in the river, it would always be thus; if one fish left, it would soon be replaced by another.

Instead of wading into the river and casting to the trout, Nick sat on the bank. His thought focused on Ethan, not the trout before him. He admitted to himself why he'd come to the Metolius today, why he'd taken this trail, and why he'd stopped at the scene of his earlier failure. He needed to confront an issue that had been in the back of his mind for years: How could he forgive someone who didn't deserve it? Someone who would ridicule the act as weak and unmanly? And why should he forgive someone who would never— could never—forgive him?

The questions eddied in his mind for long minutes; then he put them aside and shifted his focus to the river and the gracefully rising trout. The fish lay deep and unseen until a mayfly, its gray wings upright like a sail, floated into view. Then the trout rose slowly from the dark water to intercept the insect. Nick saw first a shadow, then a green shape. Finally, the trout could be clearly seen just below the surface—fins spread, eyes focused on the dun barely an inch away. But instead of immediately taking the mayfly, the trout drifted downstream with it, carefully considering, perfectly in sync with the flowing river. Once satisfied, it sipped the floating dun.

Nick watched the trout take half a dozen mayflies, then let his vision become wider and softer, taking in the clear, pure, eternally flowing river. He closed his eyes and knew the river through its sounds, then let those sounds merge with the rush of the wind in the pines and the songs of the birds.

He rose and walked to the river's edge, paused, then entered the water. Instead of facing the rising trout and casting to it, he turned downstream. "I forgive you, Ethan," he said. "I forgive you."

The words seemed hollow and pointless, and he felt no better for saying them.

He thought about the last time he'd been here, about the trout he'd lost when he forced his will on the fragile 7X tippet, and about the subsequent blowup with Ethan. A new thought came to mind. He considered it carefully, almost suspiciously, like the trout drifting downstream with a mayfly—studying, wondering: yes, Ethan was deeply insecure and could be unreasonably touchy and sensitive, but Nick was the one who had acted with impatient self-will and had broken the fragile link between them.

"I am sorry," he said at last. "I am so sorry."

He kept saying it until his heart and his lips were in agreement, the words falling like rain, each drop becoming one with the river, washing softly downstream, carried away from him until they merged with all the rivers of human regret and left him, at last, in peace.

A-M-O-R

May 10: Maupin

"EARLY TOM CRUISE MOVIE," Dave Jansen said.

"How many letters?" his wife, Clarissa, asked.

Dave and Clarissa were propped up in bed—him doing the crossword, her reading a book—as was their nightly routine on days when Dave wasn't guiding fly anglers on the Deschutes River. He counted the spaces on his crossword. "Thirteen. Third letter is an S. So's the last letter."

"Might be *Risky Business*."

He wrote in R-I-S-K-Y-B-U-S-I-N-E-S-S, which fit perfectly, then laid down the puzzle and thought about the disturbing rumor he'd heard that day: Benny Moon was planning to open a fly fishing store in Maupin. The town already had two fly shops, one of which was Dave's. Each had a dedicated but limited clientele—a Risky

Business in the best of times. Another fly shop would turn it into Mission Impossible.

He decided not to tell his wife; she would find it worrying. Besides, it was just a rumor. But if it was true ...

THE NEXT MORNING, DAVE looked out the window of his shop, which faced Main Street, and saw Benny Moon walk by with Ed Salter, a local realtor who handled both commercial and residential properties.

It was a slow morning, which was not unusual for early May, so Dave had time to ponder his would-be competitor. Benny Moon was a third-generation Korean American in his late twenties who often came to Maupin during the spring and fall for the fly fishing; winters he taught skiing at Crystal Mountain, and summers he worked for Adventure Bound, an outdoor program for teens. So he had the outdoor, boating, and fishing knowledge to succeed as a guide and run a small fly shop.

Further, Benny was focused and tenacious. Dave had once inquired about the tattoo on Benny's right shoulder: they were Korean characters that translated to "Where there is a will, there is a path."

But most of all, Benny had family money—an asset that Dave certainly lacked. Benny's father was a prominent heart surgeon in Seattle, and Benny was supposed to follow the same path as his two elder brothers: go to medical school after getting his chemistry degree. Instead, Benny opted for a gap year to go skiing, rock climbing, mountain biking, and fly fishing. One year had expanded into seven, with no end in sight. Dave could see where Benny's parents might be wondering when their youngest son was going to stop living out of a camper van and find a respectable career. A fly shop might be a grudging solution.

So Benny had knowledge, drive, motive, and family capital. He might make a go of a combined retail and guiding business. Or, more likely, there wouldn't be enough business for three shops, and they would all struggle until one or two of them went under—and it probably wouldn't be Benny.

Dave stroked his thick, dark beard. What could he do to refocus Benny Moon?

Then it hit Dave like an arrow through the heart: Benny needed a girlfriend! Nothing was more distractive to a late-twenties man than a serious love affair. Fit and handsome, Benny was popular with women—and vice versa. But steady relationships weren't part of his pattern. How could Dave make Benny fall in love? And with whom?

The shop's door made an electronic bing-bong, and two people entered. Dave knew them both and knew they weren't together but had just happened to enter at the same time.

"Good morning, Tricia!" Dave said. "Good morning, Steve. How's fishing?"

Steve Schultz, a local man, went on for ten minutes about yesterday's fishing trip—where he'd caught trout, what flies he'd used, and many other details of interest primarily to himself. Dave listened politely (for fly shop owners, listening to fishing stories is part of the job) and made a show of admiring Steve's photos. Meanwhile, the other customer—Tricia—said nothing.

If Benny Moon had a female counterpart, it was Tricia Snodgrass. Her mother was some sort of executive at Nike's corporate offices in Beaverton, Oregon. Her father never appeared in her conversation, so Dave had concluded he was out of the picture. Tricia had graduated from Reed College in Portland with a degree in psychology but had not, as originally intended, pursued a career as an academic. Instead, she helped run a cross country ski school at Mount Bachelor in the winter, guided youth adventure programs in the summer, and filled the off seasons with fly fishing, backpacking, and running. She was lithe but had extraordinary endurance and an enviable strength-to-weight ratio. Tattoos covered both arms from wrist to shoulder. Her short, spiky hair could be tinted pink, purple, red, orange, or blue, depending on her mood; this was an orange day.

Steve Schultz finally finished telling Dave about his fly fishing triumphs. After buying two flies, he turned to Tricia and asked, "I saw you around Grassy Camp yesterday. Did you do well?"

"I had a pleasant day," she said guardedly. Dave knew this to be her standard response. She was a good fly angler and had probably done better than Steve.

"I saw Benny Moon near Mecca Flat," Steve said. "He was releasing a big trout." Steve shook his head. "That guy always seems to know which fly to choose."

Dave sucked in his breath. Steve was famously clueless and hadn't twigged what everyone else in Maupin knew: never mention Benny Moon to Tricia, and vice versa.

"Of course he's smart about fly choices," Tricia said. "He's kind of a fly brain."

"What?" Steve said. Then he chuckled, "Oh, I get it."

"Actually," Tricia mused, "that's not surprising. I believe his brain is pretty close to his fly. He seems to do much of his thinking with that part of his anatomy."

"Oh?" Steve said, looking confused. "Oh, right!" He laughed nervously. "Well, he does have an eye for the ladies!"

"Yes," Tricia said. "He's God's gift to women. Except I think I'll take that present to the Returns counter: 'Excuse me, Sir, but this gift is *defective!*'"

The door bing-bonged, signaling another visitor. It was Benny Moon. *Incoming!* Dave thought to himself; he was tempted to duck behind the counter.

"Ah, the Queen of Disdain!" Benny said when he saw Tricia. He put a leg forward, doffed his baseball cap, and bowed deeply with a sweep of his arms, Renaissance style. "Your Gracelessness!" he said with mock reverence. "Dave," Benny said, straightening, "do you still book travel to foreign fly fishing destinations? Distant lands with monster fish?"

"Yes—"

"What are the farthest places from here? Show me the brochures."

Dave handed him a stack of literature.

Benny passed them to Tricia. "Your Lowness," he said, "I think you should go fishing." He tapped a photo of a taimen, a giant Asian fish. "Mongolia is a good place. Need a ride to the airport?" He turned to Dave. "I think I'll come back when you've had a chance to fumigate." He opened the door, then turned to Tricia and gave another bow. "By your leave, your Malignity."

"You don't have to *buy* my leave," she said. "I'll *give* it to you! Here!" She flipped her middle finger at him.

"Do those two not like each other?" Steve said quietly to Dave.

Dave relaxed when the shop cleared out, but his mind kept coming back to Benny and Tricia. They had so much in common and seemed like a perfect match, except for that thing of hating each other.

LATER THAT DAY, HANK O'LEARY came in. Hank was a professional fly tyer and a major supplier to Dave. He was accompanied by a short woman; he introduced her as Jackie. She browsed the women's clothing racks while Hank and Dave did their business.

After he'd written Hank a check for fifty dozen flies, Dave said, "Hey, Hank, how well do you know Benny Moon and Tricia Snodgrass?"

"I know them a little."

"How come they've never had a relationship? They're so much alike; you'd think they'd get along like ketchup and french fries."

"Maybe they did have a relationship," Hank said. "Last summer they both worked for that Adventure Bound group—the folks that run combined rafting and rock climbing trips for teens. They did several trips together early in the season. I saw them a couple of times when I was floating through from Trout Creek. They were always joking and seemed real friendly—enough that I said to myself, 'I wonder what those two are doing when the kids aren't looking?'"

"So they were together all summer?"

"They were teamed up at the beginning of summer. By the end of summer, though, they were running different groups of kids. And they'd started doing that bickering thing." He shrugged. "You have to wonder what happened."

Jackie wandered over to Hank and hung on his arm. Hank said to her, "Dave was asking about two people who are ideally suited to each other and seemed to get along once, but now they're at each other's throats."

Jackie shrugged and said, "Maybe they had a relationship that went wrong, and that's why they're nasty to each other."

"I hadn't thought of that!" Dave said. "How do you get people like that back together?"

"I don't think you can!" Jackie said. She looked thoughtful, then added, "I shouldn't be so quick. Sometimes people who really care about each other can get their feelings hurt. Then they fall into a habit of taking potshots at each other. What they're really saying is, 'You hurt my feelings, so I'm going to hurt yours!' It wouldn't bother them if they didn't care."

THAT NIGHT, DAVE AND CLARISSA sat propped up in bed, him doing the crossword and her reading. "Started a fire again," he said. "Five letters."

"*Relit*," his wife replied, not looking up.

Dave wrote in R-E-L-I-T, then put down his pencil. "Do you think …. Do you think that two people … a man and a woman … can love each other secretly and not be able to ... to admit it to each other? Or to themselves?"

"Maybe," she said, still not looking up from her book.

"Even if they're always calling each other names and ... you know ... saying nasty things about the other in front of other ... you know ... people."

His wife put down her book but didn't look at him. "What the hell are you going on about?"

"Benny Moon and Tricia Snodgrass."

She picked up her book and resumed reading. "Oh. Them."

"I wonder if there's a way to get them together. Romantically. It's possible they used to have a relationship."

"I think," she said, still focused on her book, "that you should stay out of someone else's love life."

Dave rolled so he was facing his wife. "What if Benny thought Tricia was secretly in love with him? And vice versa. Would that change things? How, they ... umm ... viewed each other?"

She put her book down again and faced him. "I love you, honey, but you know a lot more about fly fishing than you know about women. And you know a lot less about Tricia and Benny than you think."

A COUPLE OF DAYS LATER, Benny Moon came into Dave's shop to buy some flies. "I was thinking of fishing along the access road today," Benny said. "Between Nena and town. Has that stretch been fishing well?"

"Good enough."

Twenty minutes after Benny left the shop, Tricia Snodgrass came in and bought some leader material. "I'm sticking close to town today," Tricia said. "I thought I'd fish some of the backeddies below Nena."

Dave thought about directing her to another part of the river, since Benny Moon would be in that same area. Then he had an inspiration. "Great idea," he said enthusiastically. "If I was fishing today, that's exactly where I'd be! In fact, I might just float that stretch this afternoon—fishing the other side, of course, so I won't be in your way!"

As soon as Tricia left, Dave called Steve Schultz. "Steve! How'd you like to go fishing this afternoon?"

ON THE WAY TO THE NENA boat ramp, Dave told Steve his plan.

"Damn!" Steve said. "I thought you were taking me fishing out of the goodness of your heart. Now you're making me work."

"It's not work. Just follow my lead, and you'll get a nice half-day of guided fishing. Free!"

They hadn't drifted far when Dave spotted Tricia's car parked along the access road. He saw her casting close to the trees in a backeddy. "Showtime!" he whispered to Steve. "Pretend you don't see her, and follow my lead."

As his driftboat neared Tricia, Dave turned it so their backs were to her.

Steve said in loud voice, "Poor Benny Moon. That guy is hopelessly in love."

"A little quieter!" Dave whispered at Steve. "Act natural." Then in a normal voice, "In love? Who with?"

"Tricia Snodgrass," Steve said. "He's head over heels for her, but she keeps abusing him."

"But he's always nasty to her!"

"It's his competitive nature. He feels obligated to dish out as much to her as she gives to him. But the other day he told me that he wanted that whole bickering thing to stop, but he doesn't know how. You know how guys are—they don't want to appear weak."

"I can understand that," Dave said. "But he's really hurting?"

"Totally! He's all ripped up inside. Doesn't know how to express his true feelings."

"I guess one of them has to stop the cycle," Steve said.

A mile downstream, he saw Benny Moon's van; Benny was a hundred yards downriver, working a nymph along a current seam. He was shaded by overhanging alder branches and hard to see. If Dave hadn't been looking for him, he might have missed him.

When they were close, Dave whispered, "Go!"

"I'm feeling really bad for Tricia Snodgrass," Steve said.

"How come?" Dave replied.

"She's totally in love with Benny Moon."

Dave heard movement behind him—Benny getting deep into the trees so he couldn't be seen. "How do you know she loves him?" Dave said.

"She told my wife! They ran into each other at the grocery store. Tricia started crying, then said she was in love with Benny and she felt bad about how she was treating him. But she was too proud to stop."

"That must be hard—to keep your true feelings bottled up inside like that."

"Yeah! She told my wife that she didn't know how much longer she could stand it. She's at the breaking point."

"Unrequited love," Dave said. "Hardest thing there is."

DAVE HOPED THAT HIS LITTLE ruse would work some magic on Benny and Tricia and that he'd soon see them walking hand in hand down Main Street—if not down the aisle of a church to the tune of "Here Comes the Bride." Maybe there would be the patter of tiny feet. Twins, even! That would keep Benny busy and prevent him from opening a fly shop in Maupin.

Or not. Three days later, Benny was leaving Dave's store just as Tricia came in. They traded insults until Benny did one of his mock bows. Tricia held out her right hand with all fingers raised. Then she pulled the fingers down one by one until only the middle one was left. Benny bent over and stuck out his butt at her. She said, "Ah, the full Moon!" He pretended to blow a fart at her. She sniffed the air and said, "Kimchi?" Then they departed in opposite directions.

Dave rolled his eyes and sighed. He felt like he'd lit a fuse, but it had sputtered and died before reaching the dynamite.

TWO DAYS AFTER THAT INCIDENT, a customer walked into Dave's shop. "I need some more of those Supa Dupa Pupa flies," he said. "They were the go-to pattern on my float down from Warm Springs yesterday."

"Hank O'Leary ties those," Dave said. "It's killer when the caddis are active." They talked about fishing for a bit; then the customer said, "I stopped to fish just below Frog Springs. There were two people trying to camp there. Young guy, Asian American. And a woman, twenty something, wrist-to-shoulder tattoos on both arms, spiky hair. I think I've seen her around town."

"Really?" Dave said, trying not to appear as keenly interested as he felt; it was Tricia and Benny beyond a doubt. "So, were they … together?"

"I don't think so. One had a mountain bike; the other was backpacking." The customer shook his head. "They seemed to know each other, but it must be a weird relationship. They were yelling, mad as hell. I was hoping neither of them had packed a firearm. I figured I'd move on down the river, even though I was catching trout. I come to the Deschutes for peace and quiet, not warfare."

"Well, yeah—"

"But then they got quiet for a while. And suddenly they started laughing! Long, loud! Over and over. So I hung around for a bit, just to see where it was going. And like I said, I was catching fish. When I left, those two were sitting on a log talking to each other like they were best buds."

After the man left, Dave punched the air with his fist, exultant. There would be no third fly shop in Maupin! His plan had worked after all! He expected to see Benny and Tricia come into the shop that afternoon—tomorrow at the latest—making goo-goo eyes at each other.

But he didn't see them that afternoon, or the next day, or the next, or for the rest of the season. It was like they'd vanished from the earth.

Two Years Later

"HEY!" DAVE SAID WHEN TRICIA Snodgrass and Benny Moon walked into his shop, both clearly in good spirits. "I haven't seen you guys in … how long?"

"Two years!" Benny said.

"Two years? Wow! Time flies. What have you been up to?"

Tricia held out her left hand, wiggling it so the diamond wedding ring flashed in the light. "What do you think of that!" she said.

"Nice! I'm happy for you."

Benny held out his left hand, which also had a wedding ring. "Me too!" he said.

"Of course," Dave said, elated; clearly his scheme had worked after all! He should have had more faith.

"I'm living in Vermont," Tricia said, "but flew out for my mother's retirement party. The whole family came, spouses and everyone. Benny and I thought we'd drive over to Maupin and fish for a couple of days."

"I am so pleased. Are you finding some good fishing in New England?"

"It's not like here, but … yeah, it's okay. Although I won't be getting much in for while." She smiled sweetly. "We're starting a family."

"All right!" Dave wondered if they'd name the baby after him.

"Yes! Due in four months."

Dave took a good look at Tricia. She was as trim as ever. "A baby?" he said. "You don't look five months pregnant. Where are you hiding it?"

"I'm not the one who's pregnant. My spouse is carrying the child."

Dave couldn't help but glance at Benny's belly.

Tricia laughed. "My spouse. Melonie."

"Melonie?"

"Yes. Benny's sister."

"Benny's … sister?"

Tricia laughed again. "Yes! Benny and I ran into each other on the river two years ago—at Frog Springs—and got to talking—"

"More like shouting!" Benny said. "At least at first. Apparently Steve Schultz had started a rumor that we had the hots for each other."

"Well," said Dave, "you know how clueless Steve can be."

"At first we were pretty mad. Then it seemed funny, and we laughed and laughed. Once we'd gotten the tension out of the air, we relaxed and had a good chat for most of the night."

Dave was aware that his mouth was opening and closing like a trout in midstream.

Tricia continued. "I told Benny, 'thanks for the interest,' but I had finally admitted to myself that I was gay; I'd been having trouble accepting the fact. I apologized for the way I'd treated him and told him that I actually respected him and liked him a lot, but not in a romantic way. He was very kind and concerned. His sister, Melonie, is same-sex-oriented, so he understood some of what I was going through, especially with family—his parents had a real problem with Melonie's sexuality. Anyway, he introduced us, and we hit it off. Now we're married, and Melonie's pregnant."

Dave was puzzled by the mechanics of the pregnancy thing. His face must have betrayed him, because Benny smiled and said, "You go to a fertility clinic, select a donor, and have a simple 'procedure.'"

Dave thought a little more. "Oh. Uh ... oh! Right. Got it." He collected himself and tried to put on a normal face. "So what about you, Benny?"

"That's the interesting part," Benny said. "Tricia has a sister who's like her, but she prefers guys. Tricia introduced us, and it was love at first sight. Katrina and I live in Whitefish, Montana. I bought a fly shop and outfitter business there. We both teach skiing in the winter."

THAT NIGHT, DAVE AND HIS wife sat up in bed, him doing the crossword and her reading a novel. "I saw Tricia Snodgrass and Benny Moon today," he said. "They're both married."

"To each other? You're kidding!"

"No. Tricia's married to someone named Molina. No, *Melonie*. Another woman. They live in Vermont."

"I'm happy for them. Everyone deserves to find love."

Dave picked up his crossword, then put it down again. "She married Benny Moon's sister. And Benny married Tricia's sister, then bought a fly shop in Whitefish. He guides in the Flathead Basin and the Bob Marshall Wilderness. He's doing quite well, and he's very happy." He told her the story, including his original motivation: to keep Benny from opening a fly shop in Maupin. "Look at all these happy people," he said. "Benny, Katrina, Tricia, Molina—"

"Melonie."

"Right. And Melonie. None of it would have happened without me!"

"It wasn't exactly the result you intended."

"So? I was only trying to get *two* people together. Instead, *four* people fell in love and got married. And a baby on the way! And how many fly shops did Maupin have when I started this project? Two! How many today? Two! Mission accomplished, with extra credit. The rest is just ... " He waved his right hand dismissively. "Just details."

Clarissa shook her head. "Yup. Just details." She resumed her novel.

Dave picked up his pencil and crossword, feeling very proud. The next clue was *God of love,* four letters. He smiled. *That's obvious,* he thought, and wrote in D -A-V-E.

Family Vacation

June 10: Approaching Portland Airport

"WHAT'S YOUR FAMILY LIKE?" Jackie asked. "We're going to spend a week with your mother and brother, and you've hardly told me anything about them." She shook her head and tried not to sound peevish. "I've been with you three months, and until a week ago I didn't even know you had a brother."

Her boyfriend, Hank O'Leary, shrugged. "First, Evan is my half brother—same mother. Second, I've only met him twice. I've seen my endodontist more often." He jerked his thumb toward the back of his pickup truck, which was pulling a 25-foot camping trailer he'd borrowed from a friend. "And frankly, I'd rather have another root canal than go camping with them."

"Five days on the Oregon coast with your brother and mother. It's *family*. How hard can it be?" Hank would be rolling his eyes; she looked out the window so she wouldn't see it.

Jackie was fifteen years younger than Hank, and her full name was Jacqueline Moreau, although that was neither her given name nor how Hank introduced her. She'd been born in Saigon to a Chinese-French mother and a Vietnamese-French father. Her mother, father, and two brothers died during and after the fall of Saigon. She had no family of her own and couldn't understand why anyone wouldn't be ecstatic to spend a week camping with their mother and brother.

They were silent for the next five minutes before Hank said, "Well, my family is different."

"Tell me."

Hank chewed his lip. "There are a few things you should know. Um … My brother Evan is five foot three—about your size—fine-boned … rather delicate … uh …"

Jackie was aware that her jaw had dropped.

"And … uh … dresses kinda flamboyantly … uh … he's a … a big-shot hairdresser in Manhattan … uh … he's … uh … gay. Oh, and he's twenty years younger than me."

Jackie's eyes were closed. "Let me get this straight. You're six foot four, built like a brick wall, grew up on a cattle ranch in the middle of nowhere, did nasty combat jobs in the army, have had more women than I want to think about, live in Maupin—a town of 500 people—where you tie fishing flies for a living. And your brother is a delicate gay New York hairstylist." She shook her head. "So much for genetics!"

"We had different fathers and grew up in different places." Hank's right hand was making little circles in the air as he searched for words. "As you know, my father died when I was overseas with the army. Ma remarried and had another child. Evan. They lived in Arizona, and I didn't go out there much. Twice, actually. And they never came to Oregon. After her husband died, Ma moved to New York to be closer to Evan. She calls me every six months or so, and we talk for three minutes. My brother and I used to exchange Christmas cards—mostly because our mother insisted—but we stopped about ten years ago; Ma doesn't know that, so don't tell her." He cocked his head. "Are you okay with gay guys?"

"I have a career in the performing arts; I'd better be! You?"

"Doesn't bother me if it's only one or two at a time. Put me with a bunch of them, and I get to feeling weird."

"What about your mother? What's she like?"

"My mother? My mother ..." Hank's voice trailed off, and he shook his head. "My mother is ... my mother and I ... you'll just have to meet her. Anything I say about her might ... well, you can make up your own mind." Hank did a neck roll. "I don't know why she had to do this trip right now. Two weeks' notice! That's not much time to pull it together. We're lucky the campgrounds had some cancellations."

"Well, you made it happen. You'll be glad you did."

This time she saw Hank roll his eyes.

A FEW MINUTES LATER THEY drove into the crowded arrivals section of the Portland airport. Hank's truck and trailer took up a lot of space, and a few motorists gave him dirty looks.

Hank spotted his mother and brother on the curb with their baggage. He and Jackie got out to meet them. "Ma," Hank said to a slightly plump woman in her mid-seventies, "this is Jackie. Jackie, my mother, Dorothy."

Dorothy was on the tall side—maybe five foot ten. She gave Jackie a cordial hug, then wrapped her arms around Hank and patted his back. She stepped back and looked at him. "So good to see you, honey."

Evan offered his hand. "Nice to see you again, Hank," he said politely. Evan indicated a person next to him. "This is Martin, my partner."

Hank automatically extended a hand to Martin, a blond man of average build and conservative bearing who looked about ten years older than Evan. "This is Jackie Riviera," Hank said, introducing Jackie all around.

"Are you vacationing out this way?" Hank said to Martin. "So you could all travel on the same plane?"

There was an awkward silence. "Martin is coming with us," Evan said. "Didn't Mom tell you?"

Jackie saw Hank give his mother a hard look. "No, she didn't," Hank said tightly.

Jackie stepped between Hank and his mother and linked arms with both of them. "There's room for all of us," Jackie said sweetly. Then to Martin, "So nice you could join us, Martin."

A horn honked behind them. "Hey," said a bearded young man whose long hair spilled over the collar of his Hawaiian shirt, "you gonna move that big—"

"I'll move it when I'm good and ready, you goddam hippie!" Hank yelled at him, taking a step toward the man's car.

"Take your time!" the man said in an alarmed voice. "No rush!"

Hank jerked the luggage from the curb and dropped it roughly into the bed of the pickup. "Get in," he said. "*All* of you."

"HOW FAR IS IT TO THE COAST?" Evan asked as they left the airport. He and Martin were squeezed into the narrow jump seat. Jackie sat in front between Hank and his mother.

"It's about two hours," Jackie said over her shoulder. "I'm looking forward to this trip! Hank's shown me a lot of Oregon and the Northwest, but we haven't been to the coast yet."

"Me neither," said Dorothy.

"But you grew up in Oregon!" Jackie said.

"I lived on a ranch surrounded by cattle and a lot of sagebrush. I never went anywhere or saw anyone."

"Oh, I think you got around plenty," Hank said strongly, looking to the left, out his window.

Dorothy was looking to her right, out her window. "Eventually," she said in a quiet voice. "Eventually I got out."

Jackie turned to the back seat and spoke to Martin. "What do you do in New York?" she asked.

"I own a small restaurant," he said. "Amuse."

"Amuse!" Jackie said. "I've been there! Loved it!"

"You know New York?" Evan said.

Jackie hesitated. "Um … a bit."

"She has an apartment on the upper Eastside," Martin said. "Isn't that right, Ms. Moreau?"

For the last four months, Jackie had been lying low; Hank always introduced her as "Jackie Riviera" rather than her real name. But now she'd been "outed," so she might as well admit it to Martin and Evan. "Uh … yes."

Martin turned to Evan. "She's Jacqueline Moreau, the famous violinist."

"No way!" Evan said. He suddenly looked shocked. "And you're with my brother?"

"Sorry to blow your cover, Ms. Moreau," Martin said apologetically.

"It's okay. And call me Jackie." She put a finger on her lips. "Mum's the word. I'm incognito."

Martin and Evan both touched their lips with their fingers.

As they headed west to the coast, the three of them discussed New York restaurants, music, and what camping was like. Martin and Evan admitted they'd never been camping, nor had they ever ridden in a pickup truck. It would be their first trip to the Pacific Ocean. At first Jackie was afraid they'd be like those New Yorkers who treat everything west of the Hudson with deep condescension, but they weren't that way at all. They seemed genuinely excited about this trip.

HANK HAD RESERVED A CAMPSITE at Nehalem Bay State Park.

The sun hung low on the horizon by the time he had the trailer situated and made all the hookups.

"Let's go to the beach and watch the sunset," Dorothy said.

"It's dinnertime, Ma," Hank said. "We need to eat."

"Oh, just have a granola bar," Dorothy said. "We can fix dinner when we get back. Sunsets won't wait."

Jackie saw Hank's jaw go tight; he was about to say something. "I think that's a good idea," Jackie said before Hank could speak. She grabbed a handful of granola bars from the cupboard and gave two to Hank. "Let's walk on the beach."

Walking seemed to calm Hank down a bit. After a few hundred yards, the five of them naturally separated. Evan and Martin sat on a driftwood log, engaged in a private conversation. Hank's mother stood near the water looking at the setting sun. Jackie pulled Hank aside, and they walked along the hard sand just above the wave line. "Okay," she said quietly. "What's the deal between you and your mother?"

"What deal? We get along fine."

"Uh-huh. Right. They're going to do a postage stamp with you and your mother on it. 'Family Harmony' it will say. I think it'll be the new one-cent stamp. At least, that's all I'll give you for it. Tell me: what's up with you two?"

"Talking about it makes me angry."

"And you're so cool and collected as it is. No, I can tell when you need to get something off your chest. Is it because you weren't expecting Martin?"

Hank shook his head.

"Something to do with Evan?"

There was a short silence; then Hank said, "Yes."

"He seems like a nice guy. A little swishy, I admit. Is that what bothers you?"

"That bothers me a little, but that's not the real problem."

Jackie gave him a steady gaze. Finally, Hank sighed deeply.

"Okay, I lied," he said. "Or at least I didn't tell the truth. I told you my father died, then my mother remarried and had another child. The order was wrong. She had Evan, then remarried."

"Oh." Jackie picked up a rock and tossed it sidearm into the ocean. "That's it? Big deal!" She sighed, feeling exasperated. "And would you stop rolling your eyes?"

"Okay, okay." He did a neck roll.

"The neck rolls, too." She sighed. "I had no idea you were so prudish! Anyway, that's hardly a reason to resent Evan. It wasn't his fault!" She examined his face. He was expressionless—never a good sign; maybe eye rolls were better. "Or is there more to it than that?"

"Look," Hank said, pointing into the surf. "Seals! Might be chasing surf perch. Maybe I'll do some fishing early tomorrow morning on the flood tide."

Obviously there was a bigger story, but just as obviously Hank wasn't ready to reveal it. She would have to be patient. "Anyway," she said, "you and Evan should talk more. You're brothers."

"We hardly know each other, and we have nothing in common. What are we going to talk about? Compare the menus of fancy New York restaurants with Maupin's finest diners? Maybe we should take Evan out for a burger and fries at the OK Cafe." The OK, a Maupin fixture for many years, served only simple grilled fare. "You heard him! He's never been camping, never even been in a pickup truck. How do you think he'd feel about a three-day float on the Deschutes? Probably die of a heart attack if he saw a rattlesnake." Hank's face went into shock. "Omigawd! What if he wants me to take him on an overnight float trip!" He chewed his lip. "Do you think he'd be offended if I brought separate tents?"

"Maybe you could set up a banner over your driftboat: 'HE'S MY BROTHER, NOT MY BOYFRIEND!'"

"That wouldn't work," Hank said. "The wind would catch the sign, and ... Oh. You're being sarcastic."

"Ironic." Jackie sighed, then said, "Well, you both work with your hands."

Hank snorted.

Jackie looked at him sidelong. "You both cut hair."

Hank managed a chuckle. "I guess! Except he makes rich Manhattan women stylish, and I cut elk and deer hair to make fishing flies. Not a lot of common ground there." He pointed a finger a Jackie. "Coif!" he said. "Isn't that the fancy word for a hairstyle?"

"My," she laughed. "Listen to you sling those French words around!" It was a relief to have a light moment. At least Hank was making an effort. "I think you should find a way to talk with Evan. And with Martin! He's probably embarrassed that you weren't planning on him."

"Okay, okay. I'll try." He put on a look of mock sophistication and said, "I'll even work *coif* into the conversation."

"Fine! Now go talk to your mother," she said, pointing to the water's edge where Dorothy was admiring the sunset.

Hank looked pained and tentative.

"Just stand beside her and say, 'Pretty sunset.' Can you do that? Let me hear you practice. *Pretty. Sunset.*" She looked at him expectantly.

"*Pretty* ... Okay, okay. I'll go."

As Hank left, Evan came up to Jackie. "Uh, Ms. Moreau? Can I ...."

"Jackie. Please."

"Sure ... Jackie. Um ... can you give me a little advice?"

"Certainly."

"I don't know how much you know about Hank and me, but ... well, we're brothers, but we barely know each other and— "

"And you have no idea what to talk to him about?"

Evan relaxed a bit and shook his head. "Not a clue. We have nothing in common but our mother, and that's the one subject we avoid."

"Why?"

Tension returned to Evan's face. "I have no idea."

"Because Dorothy wasn't married when you were born?"

"It's more than that. But I don't really know what. No one will talk about it. Anyway, what—"

"Hank and I have been going to concerts and the theater. Talk about that. But don't get too intellectual."

"Hank's been going to the theater? Really?" Evan took on a mocking tone. "Isn't he afraid that will make him gay?"

Jackie laughed.

"Oh my god!" Evan said, now deadly serious. "What if Hank wants to come to New York and have me show him around! He won't exactly … you know … fit in with my crowd."

"Don't worry. If he ever goes to New York, he'll be with me."

DINNER WAS A SIMPLE AFFAIR prepared outside. Jackie fixed corn on the cob and a fruit salad. She put Martin to work on a green-beans-and-onions dish. When Hank fired up the barbecue and put steaks on the grill, Jackie saw Evan and Martin look at each other. She guessed they weren't fans of red meat, but they didn't say anything.

Then she took a good look at Evan's and Martin's clothing. Hank had said Evan was a "fashion forward" dresser, but today he wore tan pants with cargo pockets, a plaid shirt, a fleece vest, and lightweight brown hiking boots. Everything was brand new, and the shirt and pants were ironed. Martin's clothes were similar. Apparently Evan and Martin had gone through the REI catalog, carefully studied the models, and bought subdued recreational clothing. It was probably killing them.

While grilling the meat, Hank said, "So Evan, how many women come to you to be *coifed* in a typical week?"

Evan looked startled, like he was trying to figure out if Hank was serious. He gave a cautious answer, and they moved on to how Evan ran his business. Jackie smiled; Hank was making a sincere effort. By the time dinner was served, Hank and Evan were discussing scissors.

Over desert, Evan asked, "How come you don't use human hair for tying flies? Why do you have to kill a deer? I could send you clippings from the salon."

Jackie tensed. Evan and Martin were probably pro gun control and anti hunting—two subjects guaranteed to get Hank riled up.

She held her breath while Hank paused and composed himself. "First," he said evenly, "I get my hair from hunters who have already killed the deer and elk for the meat." He didn't mention that he himself was often the hunter from whom he got the deer and elk hides—and a lot of duck, goose, and pheasant feathers besides. "Second, the hairs of cervids—deer, elk, moose—are hollow, so they float. That's why they're used for fishing flies."

The conversation moved on, and Jackie exhaled in relief—like they'd survived a stroll through a field of land mines.

DUE TO MARTIN'S UNEXPECTED arrival, they juggled the sleeping plans. Evan and Martin took the bed in the back of the trailer. Dorothy slept on the sofa opposite the dinette. The trailer had a pull-down awning, so Hank and Jackie slept outside on cots.

The next morning, Hank rose early and donned his fishing gear. Two hours later, he returned with a dozen silver-sided surf perch.

"Are they good to eat?" Jackie said.

"Very tasty."

"Hank?" Jackie said, pulling him close and speaking low. "Thanks for being so good to everyone last night."

"It makes combat seem like a cakewalk," Hank said out of the corner of his mouth. "I think they're waking up inside," he added, pointing a fish-laden hand at the trailer.

Jackie and Hank quickly filleted the perch before anyone could come out—Evan and Martin were probably not used to the sight of fish guts when they got out of bed.

Martin was the first one out of the trailer. He eyed the fillets. "What are they?" he asked.

"Surf perch," Hank said.

Martin sniffed the fillets and looked them over carefully. "Fresh from the market?" he asked.

"Fresh from the ocean," Hank said. "An hour ago they were swimming."

"I can cook these guys up," Martin said, "if you don't mind. I think there's enough stuff in the trailer to do something interesting."

Hank looked at Jackie. She nodded slightly at him.

"Sure," Hank said, biting his lip. "That would be … great." He handed the fillets to Martin, who went into the trailer.

"He's not going to wreck them, is he?" Hank whispered once the door was closed. "I took a lot of waves to get those fish."

"I think you can trust him," Jackie whispered back. "He runs a restaurant. Besides, it will make him feel part of the group."

"Ah," Hank said.

AFTER BREAKFAST—WHICH HANK said was the best surf perch he'd ever eaten—they drove into Cannon Beach, a nearby tourist town, and visited the shops and art galleries. At one point Jackie pulled Evan and Martin aside and talked to them about the red meat issue. As she suspected, they preferred lighter fare. Then she talked to Hank; he was a bit disgruntled—as the son of a rancher, he couldn't understand an aversion to beef—but they worked out a menu that was suitable to all of them.

"Hank surprises me," Evan said quietly when he and Jackie were briefly separated from the others. "He has a better artistic sense than I would have expected. Some of his comments in that last gallery were very insightful."

"Working with fishing flies gives him a feel for the subtleties of color and proportion," Jackie explained. "And of course he understands good workmanship because he's a craftsman. He's not keen on non-representational art, though."

Evan nodded. "I'll stay away from that subject." He glanced sideways to where Hank and his mother sat on a bench, each of them silent and looking away from the other. "Among other issues," Evan added dryly.

Jackie followed his gaze. "Yes," she sighed. "Among other issues."

THE NEXT MORNING, JACKIE suggested an after-breakfast walk on the beach. Dorothy said she'd rather stay in the trailer and read, but the rest of them should go. They headed south down the sand spit. At one point Evan and Hank were ahead, with Jackie and Martin about a hundred feet behind. "She's not well," Martin said quietly.

"Dorothy?"

Martin nodded. "Heart issues."

"Has she told Hank?"

Martin shook his head. "Dorothy doesn't want to bring up the subject. And it's hard for Evan to talk about it. He gets upset. Any chance you could mention it to Hank?"

"Yes. Is there anything we should do?"

Martin shook his head. "Don't talk to Dorothy about it. She wants a nice vacation without being reminded of her health problems. But I think Hank should know."

Jackie nodded. "I'll put in a quiet word with him." After a few more steps, she said, "Is that why Dorothy pushed for this trip so suddenly? Trying to tidy things up?"

"She'd like a resolution with Hank. And she'd like Hank and Evan to be a little closer."

LATER THAT DAY THEY MOVED the trailer down the coast to South Beach State Park, near Newport, and went to the Oregon Aquarium. By now Martin was an accepted member of the group, and Hank was getting along well with his brother. The tension between Hank and his mother had eased somewhat, but like a dark cloud that covers the sun, it remained.

Jackie was tired of being everybody's go-between. Still, she decided to make another attempt at getting Hank to open up. While the others were viewing the jellyfish exhibit—a work of living art— she took Hank by the arm. "I want to watch the sea otters again," she said, leading him away.

Once outside, she said, "You seem to be getting along better with your mother."

Hank shrugged. "Only two days left. We're over the hump. I can hang on."

They watched the sea otters frolic for a bit; then Jackie said, "Your mother isn't well. Heart trouble. Martin told me."

Hank looked concerned. "Is there anything we should do?"

Jackie shook her head. "No. And don't bring it up; she doesn't want to talk about it. There's nothing we can do at this point except try to be understanding. It's possible she doesn't have much time left. Maybe that's why she came out here to see you. To tidy things up between you."

"Perhaps you're right. I hadn't thought of that."

"I still don't see what the problem is. So she had a baby and wasn't married. That's not such a big deal. At least these days. I suppose that back in the 70s ... "

"She was married, all right," Hank said. "She was married to my dad when she got pregnant."

Jackie stared at Hank. "You said he'd died! First you said your father died, then your mother remarried, then she had a child. Two days ago you said the order was wrong—that she got pregnant then remarried."

"Here's the timeline," Hank said. "She stepped out on Dad, got pregnant, then Dad died. Then she remarried, but not to Evan's father."

Jackie digested this. "Ah. She had an affair. Did they get divorced?"

"No. They were still married when Dad died."

Jackie felt Hank was still holding back. "How did your father die?" she asked quietly.

"Hunting accident." They were silent for a minute. "That's what they said, anyway."

"I see," Jackie said slowly. "And you don't think it was an accident?"

"Mom left the ranch and went to Prineville. And slept with about half the male population under the age of 40. Dad was pretty traditional, so when word got back to him … well, I can imagine how he felt. It was fall. He went into the Ochocos to hunt elk. Alone. And died of a gunshot." Hank took a deep breath. "He was too careful with firearms to have an accident. I never believed the coroner's report."

"And you found this out … how?"

"I was in Vietnam. They told me Dad died in a hunting accident. But when I got out of the army and came back to Prineville, I heard a few things. Most people were reluctant to talk. But some …" He shook his head. "One guy I knew from high school—he was a year behind me—couldn't wait to tell me how he'd met my mother at a bar and took her to a motel. I saw him in town, and it was like, 'Hi, Hank! Nice to see you again. By the way, I screwed your mother.'"

Jackie let out some air. "Wow! That … wow. I can understand how upset you were!"

Hank nodded. "I punched the guy." Hank slammed a fist into

his hand. "Knocked him flat, right there on Main Street. People held me back. I wanted to kill him." Hank shook his head slowly. "And you can imagine how my Dad felt—a man of his generation, born in the 20s, lived through the Depression, served in two wars. People had roles, and he'd played his. He'd have been hurt. Worse, he'd have been humiliated. Word was all over Prineville about how Pat O'Leary, toughest buckeroo in the county, had a young wife who would go down with anything in pants. Also, the ranch was failing—financially."

"But the coroner ruled his death an accident?"

"That was a kindness. The coroner had known Dad for years."

Jackie held Hank's arm tightly, and they walked in silence for several minutes. "I'm sorry," Jackie said. "For all of you. I know how close you were to your father. I can understand why you'd have been angry with your mother. But Hank, she's not well." She stopped and faced him squarely. "Reconcile with her," Jackie pleaded, "before it's too late. For her sake and for yours."

"How do you forgive the unforgivable? There's no doubt in my mind that she—her actions—caused Dad to take his own life. I can't get past that."

Jackie shook her head. She had no answer. Finally she said, "Maybe it's too soon for forgiveness. Maybe at this point you'd just be mouthing the words, and it wouldn't be sincere. But perhaps there's a ... I don't know ... some kind of middle ground. Acceptance, maybe?"

THE FOLLOWING DAY—THEIR last full day on the Oregon coast—started wet and windy. Walking on the beach was not attractive, and they'd seen everything in town that they wanted to see. The five of them were stuck in the small trailer, listening to the rain pound on the roof. Now and then a wind gust would shake the trailer.

Evan and Hank played gin rummy at the dinette. Martin sat

next to Evan reading a book. Dorothy napped on the bed in back. Jackie lay on the sofa opposite the dinette. She was exhausted and frustrated—exhausted from being the glue that held them all together, frustrated from her failure to bring Hank and his mother to an understanding of each other.

She had the sense that everyone was just biding their time, waiting for tomorrow to come so they could go back to their normal lives and not have to tiptoe around each other. Would it all be the same? Hank and his mother not talking? Evan and Hank reverting to being brothers yet strangers? She desperately wanted to know that this trip wasn't for nothing, that the progress they'd made would not be lost to old habits.

Dorothy came out of the bedroom. She looked at Hank, and her shoulders sagged. She looked old and tired, resigned. *I am not going to put up with this any longer!* Jackie said to herself.

The trailer was quiet; the rain had ceased, at least for the moment. "Come on, Dorothy," Jackie said, "bundle up, and let's go for a walk. The rain's stopped."

"I suppose," Dorothy said with minimal enthusiasm. "If you'd like." She reached into the closet for her coat and slipped it on slowly.

Jackie caught Hank's eye. "Coming?" she said.

"Well, I …"

"Coming?" Jackie said again, more strongly.

Hank's face showed a flash of recognition. "Right," he said.

Martin and Evan looked up at Jackie, who gave a slight shake of her head.

"I think I'll stay here," Martin said.

"Uh, yes," Evan said. "Me too."

JACKIE, HANK, AND DOROTHY walked on the beach with the strong wind at their backs. "I'm not going to mince words," Jackie said. "You two need to talk to each other. Dorothy, Hank told me about his father and how he died. He blames you, and he can't find a way to forgive you. But I think you both need to *communicate* with each other."

Hank turned his face away, tight-lipped and scowling. Jackie knew he was mad at her—really mad. She didn't care. Dorothy looked frightened. No one said anything; they walked silently for five minutes. Jackie wanted to sit on a log and cry.

Finally Dorothy said, "Hank, how can you forgive me when I can't forgive myself? There isn't a day that goes by that I don't think about your father and what I did to him."

Jackie slipped her arm around Dorothy's shoulder. "That's a hard thing to live with," she said.

Dorothy closed her eyes and nodded.

A thought occurred to Jackie. "How old were you when you got married?" she asked.

"Seventeen. I'd just graduated from high school."

"How old was Hank's dad?"

"Thirty-one."

"I see. How did you meet?"

"At dances." Dorothy's eyes lit up, and her face took on a fresh look—like she was a teenager again, in love for the first time. "He was so handsome! And that grin of his could outshine the sun! He was tall and lean, like Hank, and had red hair. He was dashing and polite, in that cowboy way. He treated me like a real woman, not a gawky teenager. I thought he was the most wonderful man in the world. I loved him at first sight."

"You grew up on a ranch, too?"

"Yes. We didn't have much company around. I didn't really … well, I'd never had a boyfriend or seen anything of the world."

"So you went straight from one ranch to another. From living with family to being married."

"My parents thought it was a mistake because of the difference in our ages. But Hank was born within a year, and they quieted down."

"So you were married, with a child, while you were still a teenager."

"It wasn't unusual back then, in our community."

"That must have been hard."

"Not at first. But then the sixties came along. I saw other people's TV—we didn't have one, you know; we didn't have electricity. I could see what was going on in the world. And how I wasn't part of it."

Jackie held back and let the words settle in.

"It seemed like such an exciting world! The Beatles, The Rolling Stones! I listened to their music all the time—we put an eight-track player in the truck, and I bought a battery-powered transistor radio. I'm afraid Hank's father didn't like my music very much. He was a Patsy Kline fan and couldn't understand how anyone could listen to Mick Jagger and John Lennon! Then I started going to Portland for protest rallies. Hank was in Vietnam by then, and I wanted him home desperately. I did anything I could to end the war. I thought, 'If I could just have Hank home, maybe my life would make sense again!'"

"Hank's father was a World War II vet, wasn't he?"

"Yes. He was a tail gunner in a B-17 over Europe. He flew thirty-two missions. He was in Korea, too, on ground crew. It was simple to him: when your country is at war, you do what you have to do. You certainly don't go to protest rallies with long-haired people in tie-died shirts."

"That must have been hard on him."

"It was tough on most people with his background. He couldn't understand what was going on in the country. It seemed like insanity to him! And he couldn't understand why I felt the way I did. I'd been happy as a mother, having my two men at home. But when it was just me and Hank's father, taking care of the stock and getting a little deeper in debt year after year … well, my world seemed very small." She sighed deeply. "And rather pointless."

"And so," Jackie said slowly, "you wanted to do something different. How old were you?"

"I was thirty-seven." Dorothy shook her head. "I'm not proud of the choices I made. But then, I wasn't prepared to make choices. When you're raised like I was—a rural woman in the 1930s and 40s—your life was laid out for you. You never wondered why things were the way they were. But then everything changed. It was 1972, and the world seemed so exciting, like I could throw my old life away and start fresh! I wanted to be part of the excitement! Hank thinks I went to drug parties and sex orgies. Truth was, I smoked a little weed, dropped acid once, and slept with six different men. That's pretty wild for someone who grew up like I did. I can see now how self-centered I was. I never thought about what it could do to Hank's father. Or to Hank. I missed Hank so much!"

Jackie was quiet and imagined Dorothy—this plump, septuagenarian with gray hair, wrinkled face, and sagging breasts— as a pretty, energetic thirty-something exploring the counterculture of that era. It was mind-boggling.

Hank broke the silence. "And I didn't come home after my one-year tour of duty," he said. Until that moment he'd been looking stoically straight ahead. "I stayed overseas and did even more dangerous things in Cambodia and Laos."

"I didn't see you for three years!" his mother said. "I was sick with worry. No letters for weeks at a time, not knowing if you were dead or alive, maimed or captured. And there I was, out on the ranch, with no one else to talk to. I had to do something different, or I'd go crazy!"

"I had no idea," Hank said, "how difficult it was for you. Or how I made it even harder. I'm sorry."

Dorothy began to cry softly. Jackie linked arms with the two of them, and they walked slowly back to the campsite. No one spoke,

except once Hank muttered, "Life can be pretty damned complicated, can't it?"

THE NEXT DAY WAS THEIR LAST. The storm blew out overnight,
and the sky was clear and blue. Hank buttoned up the trailer and
hitched it to the truck. They stowed their baggage in the back.

Jackie wanted one last photo, so they walked to the beach. She
set up her camera on a driftwood log and framed a picture, then
poked the self-timer button and ran beside Hank. "Okay, everybody,"
she said, "walk slowly, so the auto focus can keep up."

The five of them linked arms and walked toward the camera. A
red light flashed a warning. "Cheese!" Jackie said. And for a fraction
of a second, the camera captured an image of five smiling people at
the Oregon coast—a typical snapshot of a typical family, treading
carefully along the edge of the deep blue sea.

Uncle Cousin

Eighteen Years Ago

Grown-ups are sooooo booooooringgggg! thought Casey
Williams. He steered his bicycle over a mound of dirt, getting a little
air and pretending the jump was a lot bigger than it was. For half a
second he was flying—like Superman! Or better yet, gliding like
Batman, his favorite superhero, whose image graced the front of his
T-shirt.

His father, mother, uncles, aunts—and various people he was
somehow related to but hardly knew—sat at picnic tables shaded by
blue tarps tied between fir trees. They were discussing family history.
Boooooring! Even the yellow jackets seemed half asleep as they
buzzed over watermelon rinds, chicken bones, and half-eaten slices
of Aunt Alice's homemade goat sausage.

Casey was eleven years old—the youngest at the family
reunion—and he didn't seem to fit with anyone. His older cousins

had gone into town to see a movie, but Casey's mother said he couldn't go because it was PG-13. His sister and two girl cousins could have gone to the movie but decided to stay here. But would they do anything with Casey? Nooooo. They were huddled together, whispering and giggling and looking at teen fashion magazines. Why did girls *do* things like that?

Casey used to enjoy playing with his sister. Even though she was two-and-three-quarters years older, she could be fun—in a girl sort of way. But ever since those boob things had grown on her chest … well, she was just different and didn't want to have anything to do with her younger brother.

One more time over the jump. Could you die of boredom? Probably. Maybe in the next five minutes. They'd be sorry then!

The reunion was on a large tree farm near Hood River. His father had done some logging for the owner, a distant relation who let them use his property for reunions. There was a cool A-frame cabin where Casey and the other kids slept in the loft, and lots of big fir trees with dirt-and-gravel logging roads winding through them. But would they let Casey ride his mountain bike on the roads by himself? Noooo. They were afraid he'd get lost. As if!

His Uncle Ralph had also brought a mountain bike. This morning he made noises about going for a ride with Casey. But it hadn't happened. It would *never* happen.

He went over the jump again, looking at the grown-ups. Ralph happened to glance at Casey and catch his eye. Casey's father and Ralph talked, heads nodded, and Ralph walked to Casey.

"Casey!" Ralph said. "How about a bike ride with your Uncle Cousin?" When he was six years old, Casey was unsure how he was related to Uncle Ralph—he was Casey's father's step-sister's ex-husband—and had hesitantly called him Uncle Cousin. Ralph thought that was funny and ever after referred to himself as Uncle Cousin when he was around Casey, which was only every year or two. Casey barely knew him.

Casey thought about the offer of a bike ride. Did he really want to ride with an old man? Fifty-six! More than half a century! What if he had a heart attack? On the other hand, Uncle Ralph didn't act like an old man. He was built like a fire plug, as Casey's father often said: short but wide. He'd been a boxer in college. His broad, red face sported a bushy gray beard; at family Christmas gatherings Ralph always played Santa Claus. So that was good. Who wouldn't ride their bike with Santa? And Ralph had recently bicycled from Portland, Oregon, to Portland, Maine, so maybe he wouldn't die today.

"How 'bout it, Spacey Casey?" Uncle Ralph said. "Ready to roll?"

Casey grimaced. "I guess," he said.

As they pedaled down the gravel road, Casey moved his feet mechanically, showing no enthusiasm at all. Actually, he was having a good time, but he wasn't about to let Uncle Ralph know it. About a mile from the reunion, Uncle Ralph was in front. There was a noise, and Casey giggled. "What was that!" he said. He knew what it was but didn't want to say.

"That was me!" Uncle Ralph said. "I farted!"

Casey laughed.

"Those goat sausages your Aunt Alice brought? They give me gas. Hell, Alice gives me gas even when I don't eat her food! But at least I can go faster! Jet propelled!" Uncle Ralph pedaled harder and made a noise with his mouth. "Brrrrphh!" He shot ahead.

Casey went "Brrrrphh!" and sped up. This went on for the next mile, each one bursting ahead when he made a fart noise.

They paused at a fork in the road. "That looks like a good ride up there to the right!" Uncle Ralph said. "I think it links up with a dirt road that goes past the Fishers' hay field. Maybe we can ride that way tomorrow. No time today, though. Your Dad said to have you at the cabin by five o'clock. The big kids are getting back from the movie, and everyone's going to the creek for a swim."

Casey eyed the road on the right. There were lots of twists and turns and dips in the road. "Yeah, that looks fun!" he said. "Let's do it tomorrow!"

They turned to the left and headed back to the reunion. As they neared the cabin, Uncle Ralph sped ahead. "I'm getting there first!" he shouted. "I ate more of Alice's sausage! Brrrrrrph!"

Casey sped up. "Bffffftz! Brp! Bzzzzph!"

Ralph went even faster. "Bzzzzzzzt! Bthht! Brrrrrrrrphphphp!"

They raced for the cabin, each of them making louder and longer fart sounds. Casey won, although he suspected Uncle Ralph had deliberately slowed down at the end. They slid to a stop next to each other, raising a cloud of dust that drifted toward the food table.

Aunt Alice stomped toward them.

"Uh-oh," Uncle Ralph whispered to Casey. "We're in trouble now."

"You two!" Alice said sternly. "What was all that noise about? And raising dust around the food!" She clucked like a chicken. "Ralph, you're the biggest kid on the planet! Grow up and set a good example!"

Ralph turned to Casey and made a face of mock shame. It was all Casey could do to keep from laughing.

"Ralph!" Aunt Alice said. "I saw that!"

Casey's Dad came over and put his arms around Casey's and Ralph's shoulders. "I think it will be all right, Alice," he said in a soothing voice. "What's a picnic without a little dust on the food?"

Aunt Alice walked away, shaking her head. "Biggest kid on the planet!" she sputtered.

Ralph looked at Casey and made quiet hen-clucking sounds when Alice was out of earshot. "Buk-buk-buk-bwuuuuuk!"

Casey buried his head in Dad's side to smother his laughter. Dad gave his shoulder an affectionate squeeze.

"What do you say to Uncle Ralph?" Dad said.

"Thanks, Uncle Ralph! That was an awesome bike ride!"

Ralph smiled down on him. "My pleasure, young man. My pleasure. We'll do another one tomorrow."

AFTER SWIMMING, CASEY AND HIS cousins got some burgers at a local diner. They returned to the cabin half an hour before sunset. Instead of the usual happy, talkative crowd, he found a gaggle of concerned adults. Uncle Ralph had taken a bike ride by himself, saying he'd be back in an hour. But three hours had passed, and there was no sign of him. No one knew where he was, and it was getting dark.

Search parties were being organized. People talked in low, worried voices. Casey didn't know what to think. Uncle Ralph was his new friend, and he wanted to help find him. But what could he do? He was only eleven years old, and there were a dozen grown-ups, not counting older cousins. Cars and pickups left in different directions.

Casey's Dad was the last to leave. "Dad?" Casey asked. "Can I go with you?"

His father shook his head. "Thanks, Casey," he said, "but this isn't for kids."

"Dad? Please? I'm just going to ride along in the truck. I won't be in the way."

His father pondered for a bit, then said, "Sure. You'll be good company, and I can use an extra pair of eyes."

They drove around for a while, occasionally yelling "Ralph" out the window.

"Where did that crazy coot go?" Dad said to himself.

That started Casey thinking, *If I were Uncle Ralph, where would I go?* A thought came to him. "Dad, take that road over there." The road led to the route he and Uncle Ralph had biked earlier.

Casey's father shrugged and said, "Why not?"

They followed the bike route until they came to a fork in the road. "Turn right," Casey said. It was the fork he and Ralph had not taken, the road they planned to ride tomorrow. "Now stop," Casey said when they'd gone a hundred feet. "Let's get out and look for tracks."

Dusk was settling in, but they could still make out a faint tire track from a single bicycle. "Me and Uncle Ralph rode by here this afternoon. There weren't any tracks then."

"You might be onto something, young man," Dad said.

They drove two miles down the road, occasionally stopping to see if the bicycle track was still there. They called Ralph's name with more urgency and eventually heard a noise. It might have been a voice, or maybe just a bird. "Ralph!" they called in unison, louder.

A faint "Over here!" came from up ahead. They drove another hundred yards and found Uncle Ralph. He was sitting with his back against a tree. He was dirty and had some bloody spots. He looked scared and beat up.

"Boy, I'm glad you found me!" he said. "My front tire blew out when I was coming down a steep hill two miles back. I flipped over the handlebars and landed on some lava rock. I think my collarbone is broken, and I sprained my left ankle and my wrist. I got this far, but it's been tough going. Damn, but I'm glad to see you."

They helped Ralph into the truck, with Casey in the middle next to his Dad. Back at the cabin Dad got out his rifle and fired a single shot into the air; that was the signal for all the searchers to come back.

"I'll take Uncle Ralph to town for medical care," Dad said.

"I'll go with you!" Casey said.

His father started to shake his head, but then he said, "Yeah, you come along. After all, you're the hero! You knew where to look!"

Aunt Alice came by and looked at Ralph. She didn't speak, but her tight-lipped frown said everything.

After she left, Casey said, "Buk-buk-buk-bwuuuuuk!"

Ralph started to laugh, then went, "Oh! Oh! Ooo! Ow! Ah! Ooo!" He sucked in his breath. "That was funny," he said to Casey, "but don't tell any more jokes until they put me back together. And, uh, Casey? Thanks! A lot. That was good thinking, figuring out where I went." He sighed. "Damn fool. Maybe Alice is right."

"I don't think so, Uncle Cousin," Casey said. "I think you're pretty cool."

Dad wrapped his right arm around Casey and pulled him close. "Good work, Son," he said. "Fine thinking indeed." He tapped Casey's Batman T-shirt. "You're the hero now. Better than Batman!"

Casey snuggled into his father's side, feeling warm and good and grown-up. He wanted this family moment to last forever.

Six Years Later

CASEY STOOD BY THE WINDOW IN his room, looking out at nothing. He wore a T-shirt with an image of Kurt Cobain on the front. There was a soft tap-tap on the door of his room. "What?" Casey said in the sullen, irritated tone that had become his normal voice.

His mother poked her head into the room. "Uncle Ralph is here," she said tentatively. "He'd like to talk to you."

Casey rolled his eyes. "Whatever." He'd heard the car drive up earlier, then sounds of something happening in the basement—drilling, metal on metal, soft whuumphs. Nothing to do with him.

Ralph came into Casey's room and sat on a chair. Ralph put a duffle bag on the floor. *What was that all about?* Casey thought. He turned back to the window, looking outside and not at Ralph.

After five minutes of mutual silence, Ralph said, "Nice room. Decorate it yourself?" The walls were painted solid black, punctuated by posters of grunge rock bands.

Casey said, "So talk."

"What about?"

He shrugged. "Who cares? You're the one who wanted to talk to me."

"That's just what your mother said. I'm sure you've heard plenty of lectures. You don't need one more from me."

"Then why are you here?"

"To listen."

Since he'd rescued "Uncle Cousin" at the family reunion six years ago, he and Ralph had had a special relationship. Whatever Casey's age, Ralph knew how to talk to him. But for the last three years, and especially the last year, Casey hadn't talked to anyone about anything. He hated the person he'd become and wanted to change—especially after what happened last week. But he didn't know how to correct his life.

"What about football?" Ralph said after another five minutes of silence. "How about those Ducks!"

Casey sneered. "Fuck. The Ducks."

"So which would you rather talk about? The Ducks? Or fucking? You use the word a lot. I've heard you." Ralph pulled out a pen knife and began cleaning his fingernails. "So, you doing any fornicating?" he asked pleasantly. "Who with?"

Casey thought a minute. "Ingrid Petersen." Actually he'd never gotten below the waist with Ingrid Peterson, although he'd done it a dozen times with Mary Stinson. But half the senior class boys had done it with Mary Stinson. Other than Casey, she got the vote as the most "at risk" student in the Maupin School. He *wanted* to do it with Ingrid Petersen.

"What's she like? Blond? Brunette?"

Casey shook his head. "Kinda light brown."

"Was she in the car?"

Ah, so he finally got around to it, Casey thought. Last week he'd stolen a car and wrecked it. That was the latest in a string of difficulties—partying, vandalism, drugs—since his father died in a logging accident three years ago. He'd been cutting classes and had fallen a year behind in school. He was close to dropping out altogether—if he didn't get expelled first. His mother said he was out of control. He could see the hurt and worry in her eyes. But he didn't give a shit. And on those few occasions when he cared, the anger rushed up and dragged him back to a dark place.

The car he'd stolen belonged to a fly fisherman who was on a three-day float trip with Judd Boone, who owned the OK Cafe and the Rainbow Anglers Guide Service. The car was in Judd's parking lot. Casey broke a window, looking for change in the console, hoping for enough to score more weed from John Kincaid, a local fly fishing guide who was a dealer on the side. Instead he found a spare key and drove off. He'd had a couple of joints and was high. A few miles outside the town of Dufur, he took a turn too fast and rolled the car, totaling it.

"No," Casey said. "I was alone."

"Ah. Fastened your seatbelt?"

Casey nodded. His dad had been stern about seat belts when he was little, and he'd automatically buckled up. He'd never admit it, but the accident had scared the hell out of him.

"I suppose they want you to do more community service."

Casey nodded again, and conversation ended. Ten minutes passed. The room was growing dark. Casey was tired of this, tired of Uncle Ralph and all the other adults who'd tried to help him. So he asked the question that always ended these kinds of talks. "Why did my father have to die?"

Ralph shrugged. "What do other people tell you?"

"Pastor Bill at church said Jesus needed him in heaven. When I get to heaven, I'll understand."

"Pastor Bill? He's at that church in Madras your mother likes?"

Casey nodded.

"What do you think about what he said?"

Casey shrugged. "Whatever. I'm good with that."

"Really?"

"Yeah. Makes sense." He brushed his long stringy hair from his face.

"Really?"

"Sure." He felt his neck muscles grow tight. His fists clenched and unclenched.

"Really?"

The anger rose inside Casey until he thought he would explode. "I think it's BULLSHIT!" he shouted. His hair quivered and shook around his face, veins stood out on his forearms.

"How do you feel about Pastor Bill?"

"FUCK that asshole!" His fists clenched tighter.

Ralph held out his right hand, palm facing Casey. "Hit it," he said. "Punch my hand. Show me how you feel about Pastor Bill."

Casey slugged Ralph's palm.

Ralph had pulled back his hand to lessen the blow. "You call that a punch?" he said. "Do it again!"

Casey did it again—a harder hit.

"Stick your arms out." Ralph reached into his duffle bag and pulled out two boxing gloves. "Let's put these on before you hurt your hands."

Casey stood silent and seething, with his arms out as Ralph slipped on the boxing gloves. Hitting Ralph's hand had felt good—real good.

Ralph got two black padded mitts from the duffle and put them on his own hands. He tapped the right one. "Show me how you feel about Pastor Bill."

Casey slugged the black mitt.

"Who else?" Ralph said, tapping the left mitt. "Tell me who else."

Casey punched Ralph's hand again. "Fuck Mr. Bailey!" he said. Mr. Bailey was the school counselor.

Ralph held up both hands for Casey to hit. "Who else? Give me a combination, a left and a right."

Casey ran through a long list of people, hitting the mitts on Ralph's hands—sometimes the left, sometimes the right. He ended with "… and all the other assholes in Maupin."

"Is that all? What about your family? You left out your mother and sister," Ralph said.

Casey slammed the mitts some more.

"And who else?"

Casey hit Ralph's hands harder than before, maybe three times.

"Who was that for?" Ralph said.

Casey punched four more times.

"Who?" Ralph said.

Casey slugged at Ralph's hands again. He was breathing hard, and his cheeks were hot from the tears that rolled down them.

"WHO?" Ralph said.

"MY DAD!" Casey shouted.

"Why?"

"BECAUSE HE LEFT US!"

"Did he mean to?" He tapped the right glove.

Casey hit the glove as hard as he could. "He should have been more careful! He should have tried harder to take care of himself. I thought he cared about me more than that!"

"He was falling a tree and it barber-chaired. He died instantly. He was doing everything right. It was a defect in the tree."

Casey punched Ralph's hands some more. He didn't care that he was crying.

Ralph rose and said, "Follow me." He led Casey to the basement. A punching bag hung from a ceiling beam. Apparently that's what Ralph was doing when he first arrived.

"Hit it," Ralph said, pointing at the punching bag.

Casey hit it as hard as he could.

"Show the punching bag how you feel about your father," Ralph said, standing behind the bag and holding it for Casey.

Casey hit the bag several times.

"How do you feel about yourself and your life?"

Casey attacked the bag with a wild flurry of punches, then sat on the floor. "I know it wasn't his fault. But I can't stop feeling that way." He folded his arms across his knees and dropped his head on them.

"I'm not going to tell you it's wrong to feel that way," Ralph said quietly. "In time, though, you will come to terms with it. Until then, come down here once a day—more often if you want—and beat the snot out of this bag."

Casey nodded. "I want to be better than I've been."

"What do you think you need to do?"

He wiped his runny nose on his sleeve. "I'm going to tell my mother I'm sorry. I'm going to go to all my classes and study hard and get straight As. I'm going to buy that guy a new car. I'm going to—"

"Whoa! One thing at a time! Start with the simple stuff. What will you do tomorrow? Pick one really easy thing that helps someone else."

Casey thought for a bit. "Wash the breakfast dishes?"

Ralph nodded. "Good start. Next day, do another good thing. Just try to do one good thing a day."

A MONTH LATER, CASEY WAS in the basement hitting the punching bag when he heard a car drive up. Ralph came downstairs. He moved behind the bag and held it for Casey.

"How's it going?" Ralph asked after a few punches.

"Good," Casey said. He hit the bag several more times. "Well, better anyway." Trying to do one good thing each day helped. At first, he did it early in the day—to get it over with. Then he tried doing two good things so he could get ahead and not have to do anything the next day. But he'd come to admit that helping other people made him feel better about himself. He still had his bad moments, and he cut a few classes every week and didn't always get his homework done and smoked pot and drank a few beers. But not as much as before.

"I saw Judd Boone today," Ralph said carefully. "He's a little leery of you. As you might expect."

Casey paused and cocked his head, then resumed hitting the punching bag. It was Judd's customer's car that Casey had stolen and wrecked.

"But he thinks you're a good kid, deep down. He needs someone to clean his boats for him during the fishing season. Several times a week, maybe an hour each time. Doesn't pay much, and what you earn pays for the wrecked car. How do you feel about that?"

Casey hit the punching bag a few more times before looking at Ralph again. "So I work my butt off cleaning crap from someone else's boat," he said. "For free." He went back to the punching bag for a minute, then paused and said, "On days when I clean a boat, do I still have to do something nice for someone else?"

"That's up to you."

Casey shrugged. "Sure. Why not?"

This Year

CASEY LAUNCHED HIS DRIFTBOAT at the Nena boat ramp, then zipped his jacket over his favorite hoodie, the one with "Casey Williams Guide Service" printed on the front, along with the URL of his website and a picture of a trout. The sun was still below the rimrock, and Casey's driftboat was colorless in the faint light. It was a chilly morning, and a light mist rose from the river.

Frank, one of his clients for the day, strode up and clapped Casey on the shoulder. "You must be the famous Casey Williams, Maupin's hero of the hour!" said Frank. He turned to his friend Hal, the other client. "Do you know what our guide did last April? Ran into a burning building and saved a guy's life! That's what."

"Really?" said Hal.

"Really! Judd Boone told me all about it. This kid drove into Maupin at crack-o-dawn and saw smoke pouring out of the Drift Inn—"

"Was that the place with the world's worst hamburgers? Just down from the OK Cafe?"

"Yeah. They were god-awful." Frank put a hand on his stomach and made a face. "Anyway, Casey breaks down the door, runs in—"

"Actually," Casey said modestly, "I kinda crawled in. It was pretty smoky and—"

"See?" said Frank. "He's not only brave as hell, but he's smart." Frank put a finger on his temple. "Thinking under pressure! Got down on the floor. Under the smoke. Grabs some guy by the collar and drags him out. Saved him away from certain death!"

"Was the guy okay?" Hal said.

"Smoke inhalation," Casey said. "And traumatic brain injury. He was hit on the head by something. He's home now and ... well, he's not great, but he's getting along." He wanted a change of subject. "Gear in the back, please, and lay your rods here," he said, pointing. "Fishing's been on and off, but we had two steelhead yesterday. There's always hope!"

"Hope is all we need," said Frank.

"I'm good with hope," added Hal.

Casey carefully placed a small green duffle bag between the front seat and his footrest. "Hop in," he said, "and let's go look for some fish!"

Casey would have these two anglers in his boat today, plus his Uncle Ralph. Frank and Hal had been Casey's clients for three years. They were cheery, positive-thinking men in their mid sixties—always eager no matter how bad or good the fishing had been. They were Uncle Ralph's kind of people, so he was happy that Ralph was on this trip. Two months ago, Ralph had said to Casey, "I'd like you to do two things for me on my birthday. First, take me down the Deschutes in your driftboat." So this trip was as much for Ralph as for Frank and Hal.

TWELVE YEARS AGO, RALPH set Casey up with a job: cleaning boats for Judd Boone. Near the end of summer, Casey went on some multiday float trips as a "camp assistant," setting up tents and toting bags of gear up and down the riverbank at each campsite. He became fascinated with the river and fly fishing. Seeing Casey's enthusiasm, Judd taught him how to fish, row a boat, and negotiate whitewater. The next year, Casey rowed the bag boat for the overnight trips. In his spare time, he fly fished; he quickly became passionate and expert.

Casey rowed the bag boat for two summers. Between those gigs with Judd, he got serious about his studies—which was difficult due to his dyslexia—and graduated from high school. He even dated Judd's daughter, Megan, and fell in love with her. But after she went to college, she dumped him, causing serious depression. He got over it, moved on, and became a fishing guide. He worked on his own on the Oregon coast in the winter, and summers he guided for Judd.

Through all Casey's ups and downs, Uncle Ralph continued to be a part of his life, offering guidance and encouragement at all stages.

AS THEY NEARED THE FIRST RUN, Frank leaned to his right and let one fly. "Better out than in," he said, unapologetic. "Mexican omelet for breakfast. Love 'em, but there are side effects."

"Next time have the oatmeal," Hal said.

"Just stay away from Aunt Alice's goat sausage," Casey said. Then he added, "Inside joke," and shot a grin and a wink in Ralph's direction. He thought he heard a soft "buk-buk-buk-bwuuuk" in reply.

IT WAS A BETTER THAN AVERAGE day of fishing. Frank hooked two steelhead and landed one, and Hal hooked and landed another. They reached the take-out ramp near sunset; then Frank and Hal got in their car, waved good-bye to Casey, and drove away.

After they left, Casey quietly returned to the boat and retrieved the duffle bag from behind the front seat. He waded into the river with the bag slung over his shoulder. The west side of the canyon had a golden glow from the setting sun, and the river shimmered with the reflected color. Downstream, Casey heard the descending notes of a canyon wren. Across the river, three deer came to the water for an evening drink.

Casey pulled a container from the bag. "Well, Uncle Cousin," he said. "We took care of one of your birthday wishes. Here comes the second one." Casey emptied the container on the water.

Ralph had told Casey his two birthday wishes at the hospice center about a week before his death. The first was to carry his ashes down the Deschutes—preferably with good companions. The second wish was to spread his ashes on the river. "Make me one with the fish," he'd told Casey.

Casey watched as Ralph's ashes swirled in the current then faded from sight. "Good bye, Uncle Cousin," he said, his voice cracking slightly. "You're the real hero."

DNA

June 12, Seattle

MARTY CAMPBELL STEPPED ONTO the balcony of Seattle's Sand Point Country Club—the venue for tonight's party, his fortieth high school reunion—and admired the view. The Cascades rose to the east, the tallest peaks glowing pink from the sunset; sailboats glided on Lake Washington; golfers strode the country club's lush, hilly course.

On a warm, early summer evening like this, Seattle seemed like a slice of heaven. He relished the clean, sparkling pleasantness of it all and thought of ways he might describe his life. Happy? Satisfied? Secure? Comfortable?

All those words fit, but he decided *comfortable* best described his feelings.

For the last thirty years he'd worked at Safeco, a large insurance company headquartered in Seattle; he was now a first-level manager in the HR department and looked forward to retirement in five or seven years. He and his wife Carole were empty nesters with one married son whose wife was expecting. Their other son had recently graduated from college. Their three-bedroom, two-bath house was modest, but in a safe, decent north Seattle neighborhood; best of all, the mortgage was finally paid off. No mortgage, no kids in college, both boys on their own, grandchild on the way. Life was good! And, above all, *comfortable*. Very, very comfortable.

Marty turned, leaned his back on the railing, and looked into the room. He saw Jon who, like Marty, had been in the Roosevelt marching band. Jon was talking to a pretty lady in her late thirties. Jon pointed toward Marty, and the young woman he'd been talking to looked his way, then nodded politely to Jon and approached Marty. "Are you Marty?" she said in slightly accented English.

"Yes. Marty Campbell." He tapped his name badge, then extended a hand. She was on the short side, with dark, curly hair that hung to her shoulders. She had a lithe, athletic figure. She looked familiar, but he was sure they'd never met.

"I'm Rachael Eisen," she said politely after taking his hand. "I'm looking for people who might have known my mother. Her name was Leah. Leah Sternberg she would have been then. I think she was in your class."

That explained the familiar appearance. Rachael Eisen resembled her mother, who'd played clarinet in the band. The eyes were different, though. "Yes," he said, "I knew Leah."

"And she was in your class? Not the year before?"

"Yes, this class. I'd hoped she'd be here tonight. But she didn't come to any of the other reunions, so I'm not surprised." He gave Rachael an amused smile. "Did she send you to check up on us?"

"No. Sad to say she died last year."

"I'm truly sorry to hear that," he said, embarrassed at his flippancy. "My condolences to you and your family."

Rachael nodded a thank you, then seemed to search for words. "I understand that my mother—when she was at your high school—may have dated someone in the band. Someone named Marty. I don't know the last name." She looked at him expectantly.

"Well, she and I went steady our senior year. So I must be who you're referring to. But I'm not sharing any secrets about your mother!" This last he offered in jest.

She didn't laugh or even smile. "Did you … date for very long?"

"Oh, most of our senior year. Then part of our first year of college. We went to the same college for our freshman year. Then she moved to Israel with her parents. Is that where you're from? Israel?"

"Yes. I was born there. And live there still." She seemed unsure and a little nervous. "I'm sorry to be so forward," she said, "but there are things I'd like to know about my mother, things I didn't get to hear about when she was living. It's a … comfort to me. I enjoy hearing about family and her connections."

"I'm not sure I can help you, but what would you like to know?"

"Perhaps you could tell me when … you and my mother started dating."

"We knew each other for a long time because we were in the marching band together. But we didn't date until fall of our senior year."

"I see. And when did you break up?"

"When she moved to Israel, which was March of our freshman year in college."

"Were you and my mother … close?"

Marty was suddenly on guard. He and Leah had been close—very close, sexually close. He'd never talked to anyone about that part of their relationship. Back then you didn't go around telling people such things—at least Marty didn't—and he wasn't about to start now, especially with Leah's daughter. He made an offhand gesture. "Close? Oh, you know. We were just kids. I'm sorry to hear she passed on." He wanted to end the conversation, so he looked at his half-empty glass and said, "Excuse me, I'm going to get a refill. Nice chatting with you."

He started to turn away, but she took his hand and prevented him. "This is very important to me," she said in a low, serious tone. "Please talk to me about my mother. Just for a moment."

Marty stopped. This conversation was making him uncomfortable, but he felt sorry for the young woman. "How can I help you?" he said.

Rachael Eisen moistened her lips and searched for words. Finally she said, "I was born six months after my mother immigrated. I'm thirty-nine years old." She let that sink in, then added, "I was born in mid-September."

Marty stared at her, stunned.

"I weighed seven and a half pounds at birth," she said into the silence.

In other words, she was a full-term baby who was born six months after Marty and Leah broke up.

Marty felt dizzy and wanted to sit down, but sitting down would have prevented escape, which was what he wanted most of all. "I'm afraid I really can't help you," he said quickly. "I really can't help you at all. I'm sorry about your mother's passing. Excuse me, but my wife is coming." His wife was halfway across the room, deep in conversation with someone else.

Marty started toward his wife, but Rachael followed him and grabbed his arm. "Please," she said desperately. "It's very important to me. Please talk to me. I'm in Seattle for two more weeks. Please!"

"No, won't work! I'm leaving tomorrow for a two-week fishing trip. No cell coverage. Sorry. Sorry." It was an exaggeration; he'd only be gone four days.

"It's very important to me," she said again. She pressed something into his hand. "I know this is a hard thing for you. I can see that you're uncomfortable. But … call me! Please."

As Marty neared his wife, Rachael stopped and let him go. Marty looked in his hand; she'd left him her business card. He stared at the card, which had her name; a phone number, obviously foreign;

a post office box in Tel Aviv; and her job title: Journalist. A local number—probably a prepaid cell—was written in the corner. He stuffed the card in a pocket.

The flowing reunion crowd obscured Rachael Eisen, but Marty could see his wife staring at her.

"Who is that?" his wife said.

"No one. She thought I was somebody I'm not."

EARLY THE NEXT MORNING MARTY headed east on Interstate 90. A couple of hours later he launched his small, one-person pontoon boat on an upper section of the Yakima River. He floated downstream, occasionally pulling on the oars to maintain his position or to work through a minor rapids. When not rowing, he cast his five-weight fly rod, aiming a Clarks Stonefly toward the riverbank.

Fly fishing was Marty's favorite recreation. He looked forward to doing more of it when he retired in a few more years. But for now he had to be content with short trips like this one.

The golden stonefly hatch was still on. The big insects hang out in bankside trees and grass stems, where they look for mates. They often lose their grip and drop onto the water. At the sight or sound of a splash, an observant trout pounces on a hapless insect.

The stonefly hatch can be tricky. Your fly needs to land close to the bank or be directed under overhanging trees. Too far out, and you miss the fish. Too close, and your fly ends up in the grass or dangling from a branch.

Unfortunately, Marty was distracted and preoccupied today, so his casting was not up to his usual high standard. He tried to focus on fishing, but his mind would think of nothing but Rachael Eisen and her mother, Leah Sternberg. Was it possible he was Rachael's father? That seemed to be what she was getting at.

He and Leah had attended Theodore Roosevelt High School in northeast Seattle. Roosevelt was an excellent, even exceptional, public school. It gathered students from neighborhoods that ranged from upper-middle-class Laurelhurst to less tony areas. At that time—forty years ago—Roosevelt had almost three thousand students, and if you looked hard you might spot a few dozen black faces and even a smattering of Jews.

Marty had occupied the center of the student spectrum, a WASP boy from the middle of the middle class, living in a modest house on a pleasant tree-lined street within walking distance of Roosevelt. He pulled down better than average grades but nothing that would land him on the honor roll.

He'd not been one of the elite, but, thanks to his naturally sunny disposition and joke-telling skills, he'd gotten along with most people. It helped that he was tall and good looking, with a fresh, perpetually boyish face, and had no socially unacceptable quirks.

He'd played no sports and joined no clubs. However, he was not, in Roosevelt parlance, a Teddy Leftout because he was in the marching band, where he played tenor saxophone and had many friends.

Every Friday in the fall, the band kids had donned their green-and-yellow uniforms, filed into a bus, and traveled to the football games. There they rooted for the Roughriders, played the fight songs, and put on a halftime show. A subset, including Marty, showed up at winter basketball games and played jazz tunes during time-outs. No one thought of the band kids as cool, but they constituted a group where mild nerdiness was acceptable, even valued.

His relationship with Leah had begun innocently enough. One October night after a football game, Marty and Leah—who played clarinet—went to a local teen hangout, The Burgermeister. Although Marty was friendly with her, they'd never dated. And technically this wasn't really a date since there had been no planning; he was simply giving her a ride home after the game. Both were hungry, so they'd stopped for hamburgers and milkshakes.

But conversation had been easy and fun, and after leaving The Burg they drove around a bit, just to keep things going. When they passed Golden Gardens, a big park on Puget Sound, Leah suggested they drive into the expansive parking lot. Many cars were lined up facing the water, and in each car there was a young man and a young woman making out—sometimes one pair in the front seat and one pair in the back seat. In local teenspeak this was referred to as "watching the submarine races."

After Marty had parked the car, he and Leah wrapped their arms around each other and kissed for half an hour; then he drove her to her home.

The next week had been a repeat, except this time she took his hand and placed it on her breast. Marty had no objections to this escalation, and Leah seemed to enjoy it. He sensed that she'd been down this path before. Marty, on the other hand, had never had a regular girlfriend and didn't have any experience with such things. He liked it.

Within two weeks they were inseparable—deeply "in love." Marty was a bit confused about the difference between *love* and *making out*, but making out was exciting, so he chose to believe he was in love.

By the end of November Marty had mastered the art of unbuttoning a blouse and unhooking a bra with one hand, and not long after they were reaching down each other's pants. In early January of their senior year, they jettisoned their virginity.

For the rest of the school year they'd tumbled along in a rush of sexual discovery. After high school, they both attended Western Washington State College in Bellingham, which gave them more privacy than living at home.

But by February of their freshman year the relationship had begun to fray. Then Leah abruptly announced that she and her parents were moving to Israel. She was gone in less than a month.

Marty had known that Leah was Jewish, but they hadn't talked much about it. Her parents were not especially religious. They were cultural and social Jews, something that Leah had to explain to Marty, who thought being Jewish was a question of religion, like being a Presbyterian. Leah's parents were also ardent Zionists—another subject Leah had to explain to him.

He and Leah promised to write, but their correspondence ceased after three letters. Marty moved on and figured Leah had done the same.

The sexual aspect of their relationship had been surprising to Marty. Not that he hadn't expected to enjoy it: after years of thinking, talking, dreaming, fantasizing, and, not to put too fine a point on it, *practicing* sex, he found the actual experience of it even better than he'd imagined. That came as no revelation.

The surprise was how much Leah had liked it. In fact, Leah initiated every sexual escalation. Marty was never resistant, but Leah always led the way.

However, with forty years of hindsight he could see why their relationship hadn't lasted. Sex and marching band were mostly all they had in common. Perhaps they could have grown closer in other ways, gotten to know each other's minds as well as they knew their bodies. But they'd rushed into a physical relationship that dominated everything.

AFTER A DAY OF DISTRACTED AND therefore mediocre fishing on the Yakima, Marty drove to Maupin, Oregon, on the Deschutes River. He was going to spend a day with Judd Boone, his favorite fly fishing guide, then fish on his own before heading back to Seattle.

Marty and Judd launched at the Warm Springs boat ramp. The fishing was similar to the Yakima except there were more caddisflies than golden stoneflies, and they couldn't fish from the boat. Although Marty still had trouble concentrating, he landed some nice trout before they broke for lunch.

"Great morning!" Marty said to Judd as they ate their sandwiches on the shore.

"They're on the grab today," Judd agreed.

The morning's success, combined with Judd's good company, put Marty in a better, more comfortable, frame of mind. He decided to share—obliquely—his concerns with Judd, a man whose advice he'd always respected. "I had an interesting conversation with a friend," Marty said, reaching for an apple. "My friend had a young woman come up to him and hint that she might be his daughter. My friend had had an intense relationship with the young lady's mother in high school and for most of his freshman year of college."

"What did your friend do?"

"He ran off like a scalded dog before he could find out."

"Was he your age?"

"Yes. It was at our fortieth high school reunion. He was a classmate."

"Wow. That would kinda scare a guy. There you are thinking about retirement, and some stranger walks up and says, 'Hi! Are you my daddy?'"

"Yes, my friend was quite confused. Perhaps he did the wrong thing. What would you do? If you found yourself in that situation?"

"I'd say, 'Lady, that would have been an immaculate conception.' I was a late bloomer. The flesh was willing, but the spirit was weak."

"What do you think my friend should have done? Or, given that he blew it on the first pass, what should he do now?"

Judd looked thoughtful. "Does your friend have a way to contact the young woman?"

"She left him a business card."

"I guess you'd … I mean, your friend would … need to consider several things. First, is this woman on the level? She could be a con artist; this is not an unusual scam. So I'd do a background check—look for arrests, aliases, that sort of thing. See if she's real. There are agencies that do these things for a modest fee."

"Good idea. I hadn't thought of that."

"I'll give you a name; we sometimes do background checks on new employees."

They fished the rest of day, then loaded the boat onto the trailer at the Trout Creek ramp and headed back to Maupin to have dinner at the OK Cafe, which was owned by Judd's family.

When Marty came in the door, he did a double take. "Judd! You've put in an espresso machine! How twenty-first century of you." Marty immediately ordered a latte from the barista, a young woman of eighteen or nineteen. A fortyish man—her father?—sat in a chair next to her, engrossed in a book.

"Hey, Logan!" Judd said to the seated man. "How's the guidebook coming?" He turned to Marty and said, "This here's Logan McCrea. He's writing a guidebook about the Deschutes. Giving away all the secrets!" Judd pushed up McCrea's book so he could see the cover. "Ah, not the guidebook. You taking the day off? *For Whom the Bell Tolls.* Hemingway! 'No man is an island entire of itself … something something … a part of the main … blah blah blah … So …'" Judd paused and looked thoughtful.

"So do not ask for whom …" Marty interrupted. "I had to memorize that poem in high school."

"Right!" Judd said. "No man is an island, entire of itself, blah blah blah, So do not ask for whom the bell tolls, it tolls for thee."

"Close," Logan said, returning to his novel.

While Judd and Marty waited for their food, Judd said in a low voice, "I'd say the next thing to think about are the family considerations." He stopped. "I'm talking about your friend. The guy at the reunion."

"My friend said the young woman's mother had passed on."

"Ah. But there might be a father—an adoptive father or

stepfather that's still in the picture and feels close to her. He could be very hurt if he learns she's checking out her birth father."

"Hmmm."

"Also, she might have siblings who would be offended. Then there's your … friend's … family. How would they feel about a long lost sister?" Judd gave Marty a serious look. "And how would your friend's wife feel about it?"

"Lots to consider."

"Yup."

MARTY FIDGETED AT A TABLE in the back of Coffee Diva in Seattle's north end. He'd bagged his last day of fishing on the Deschutes; instead, he'd followed Judd Boone's advice and arranged a background check on Rachael Eisen, paying extra for a 24-hour rush request. She was on the level, as far as anyone could tell. Any minute she was going to come through the door, and he was going to talk to a stranger who was probably his daughter.

He carefully arranged three swizzle sticks, precisely lining them up. Then he put one on top of the other. Then made a triangle and drummed his fingers next to it before checking his watch. Only one minute since the last time he checked? Seemed like longer.

He'd discovered that Rachael Eisen was famous, at least in certain circles. A few Google queries revealed that she was a prominent Israeli journalist, well known for her hard-hitting investigative reporting. She was freelance and wrote as a correspondent for several Israeli newspapers as well as the *New York Times*, Reuters, and the *Christian Science Monitor*. She also did some TV work for CNN and BBC. Her even-handed reporting on the plight of both Palestinians and Israelis had earned respect—and powerful enemies on both sides.

She entered the coffee shop, and he raised a hand. She waved back, ordered a coffee drink, and came to the table. Marty pushed the swizzle sticks to one side.

"Thank you for meeting with me," Rachael said. "I know this is an uncomfortable thing to consider."

Marty spread his hands. "We should talk. Like you said, it's important. What did your mother tell you about me?"

"Nothing. She never mentioned you. The story she told me—and my grandparents always corroborated—was that she'd married when she was twenty. Her husband was in the Army and was sent to Viet Nam, where he died in combat. So she was a widow 'with child.' She even had a photo of some GIs in Viet Nam and said the guy on the left was my father. God knows where she got the photo. They were all heartbroken at her tragic loss—the story went—and came to Israel to make a fresh start. Two years later, my mother married my father—my stepfather—who raised me. But the dates didn't work out."

"What do you mean?"

"When I was thirteen I saw my mother's passport. Her birth date was a year later than what they'd told me. I asked about it, and my mother said the government got the date wrong, but it was too much hassle to fix it. When I went to university and learned some research skills, I got a copy of her birth certificate. The birth date was the same as on the passport. So I knew she'd lied. Then I looked up my own birth certificate. It listed her maiden name and no name for the father. Then I checked US military archives and found no record of my 'father.' So it was all a big story."

"Did you talk to your mother about it?"

She shook her head. "It would have caused problems with my stepfather, and I cared very much for him. He died fifteen years ago—pancreatic cancer. I waited another year, then asked my mother what was up. She said it was a long time ago, and I should leave it alone. So I did. Until now. I had to come to Seattle for a story I'm researching on US military sales to the Middle East. l extended my stay so I could check out my mother's history."

"How did you track me down?"

"It was totally by chance. I met someone who'd moved to Israel from Seattle. She was the right age, so I mentioned my mother's name, figuring she might have run into her in the Jewish community. Turns out she remembered my mother. They saw each other at bar mitzvahs when they were in their teens. That was one of the few religious things my grandparents did—there was a party involved, and they were very social people. So I casually asked this woman about boys my mother had dated in Seattle. She said she remembered my mother talking about a gentile named Marty who was in the high school marching band. She couldn't remember which school."

"That's a tenuous lead—a gentile from a high school band in Seattle."

"I've dealt with worse leads than that! Anyway, I called Seattle high schools to find out where my mother graduated. I knew the year—or two years, if my mother's version was true, which I was sure it wasn't." She pushed her hair back from her eyes. "So I tracked her down to Roosevelt and your year. Then I tried to find band members with a first name of Marty. The administration didn't have a record of that, but they told me there was a reunion of her class coming up at the end of the week. So I showed up."

"Wow! You know how to do research!"

"Well, I'm an investigative journalist. As these things go, it was pretty easy."

"Rachael, let me be frank."

"Please do."

Marty took a deep breath. "It's possible I'm your father. Your mother and I had … relations … for over a year, starting in high school and ending when she moved …"

"I always thought my mother might be a bit … sexually aggressive, shall we say. Was she?" Rachael looked expectant and slightly amused.

"Well ..." Marty examined the ceiling, then the rest of the room, and finally turned back to Rachael. He cocked his head and spread his hands.

"I'm not surprised," Rachael said. "I bet she initiated most everything."

"Uh ... uh ... okay, yes. She did."

"So it wasn't like you seduced her or anything. Maybe more the other way around." She looked him full in the eyes. "I'm sorry. I'm making you uncomfortable, aren't I?"

She was, but he didn't say so.

"It's the journalist in me," she said. "I tend to be blunt and sometimes ... a bit pushy. I'm used to digging into things from every angle. Forgive me."

Marty was warming up to this intelligent, forthright, and evidently fearless young woman. To think that he might have sired such a daughter—amazing!

"How was your relationship at the end?" she asked.

"Frankly ... it was going downhill. If she hadn't moved to Israel we probably would have broken up pretty soon."

"Which explains why she wouldn't have pushed you to marry her. Do you know if she was seeing anyone else at that time? On the sly?"

Marty had never considered that before. Could Leah have been stepping out on him? "Not that I know of."

"But it's possible, given how my mother was at that time. And that you weren't getting along."

"I suppose so."

"A DNA test would prove paternity," Rachael said. "Are you okay with that?"

"I ... I ..."

"Let me tell you why it's important to me. I'm not just being nosy. Yes, it's closure, of a kind. But ... " She dropped her journalistic edge, and her voice grew softer. "I've lost everyone around me—my mother, stepfather, grandparents. I have no siblings. I was married, but we divorced and don't speak. No children. But I've always felt that family is important, and I … I'd just like to know if there's someone else out there. My work takes me to dangerous places, violent people. There's some small comfort knowing that somehow, somewhere, I've got family."

Marty began to grasp why this mattered to Rachael. But a second thought came. "There are more people involved than just the two of us. I have a wife, two sons, and—"

"I'm not looking to insert myself into your family's life," she interrupted. "I'll continue to live in Israel, and you would see me rarely, if at all. I just … would like to know … there's someone out there I'm connected to."

"It's not just that. I have their feelings to consider. My wife knows nothing about you. This will come as a big shock to her. I need to talk to her first."

Rachael nodded. "I see. That's very thoughtful of you. I can tell you're a kind and considerate person."

Marty shook his head. "Not especially."

"Don't deny it," Rachael said. "My mother might have been a hotpants, but she was a good judge of character. She liked you for a reason." She sipped the last of her latte and looked apologetic. "I don't want to imply that I thought my mother was … well, slutty. I doubt very much that she ever cheated on my stepfather. But after he was gone—I was in my twenties by then—she had a string of boyfriends. She could be flirtatious." Rachael gazed into her empty latte cup. "Please talk to your wife and let me know. Soon."

They got a second round of lattes and spent the next hour talking about Rachael's career. As she explained her work, Marty became aware that he knew next to nothing about what was going on in Israel, the Middle East, and indeed the rest of the world. Sure, he watched the network news shows—sometimes—but as for the real issues and their complexities, he was quite ignorant.

Rachael had spent years reporting on the Middle East. Lately she had focused on the plight of Palestinians in Gaza and the occupied territories (Marty wasn't aware that the territories were "occupied") and in old Jerusalem. But she also reported on security issues and terrorism. Marty realized he had no appreciation for the Palestinians' frustration, nor for how deeply threatened Israelis felt. "People on both sides," Rachael said, "only want to see things from their own point of view. That's where I come in: I try to explain it factually and objectively. There are a small number of people ... " she held her thumb and forefinger half an inch apart "who want to hear the truth. Just enough to keep me employed. Everyone else ... " she spread her hands far apart "would like me to go away."

"Why?"

"Because most people don't like it when you challenge their prejudices. They divide the world into good people—themselves—and bad people—everyone who isn't like them. I show how we're all human, all part of the whole, and that we need to care about each other. A lot of folks don't like to hear that."

When they parted, Marty felt unsettled, and not just because Rachael was probably his daughter. Learning about her work had disturbed him. All his life he'd striven to get along with others, to avoid conflict, to achieve a high measure of security for himself and his family. But in the process he'd lost track of how he was connected to the rest of the world. He felt uncomfortable with himself and what he'd become.

"YOU MIGHT HAVE A DAUGHTER?" Marty's wife Carole said. "Might?"

Marty nodded sheepishly. "My high school and freshman girlfriend. Leah Sternberg. She had a child six months after we broke up. She'd moved to Israel, so that's why I never heard about it."

Carole pursed her lips. "Is it Rachael Eisen? That journalist who was talking to you at the reunion?"

"Wha … how do you know about her?"

"You left her card on the dresser. So I Googled her. Also, I've seen Leah Sternberg's photo in your Roosevelt yearbook. Rachael Eisen looks just like her."

"You looked up my high school girlfriend in the yearbook?"

"Duh!"

"Really?"

"Come on. Don't you know anything about women?"

"Sometimes I think not. Anyway, she does look a lot like Leah. Except for the eyes."

"Yes. That's because she's got your eyes. Leah's face and hair, your eyes."

"I knew they looked familiar. I'm not very good at being sneaky, am I?"

"Hopeless. But it's one of your most endearing traits. So what are you going to do? Have you talked to her?"

"Yesterday, at Coffee Diva. She'd like us—me and her—to do a DNA test. I said I needed to talk to you and the boys."

"What does she want? It's not some sort of con job, is it?"

"I had an agency do a background check."

Carole nodded. "Good move. And she checks out online. But you never know—it could be someone who resembles Rachael Eisen and is posing as her. All you have is a business card; they're easy to make."

Marty hadn't considered this angle. "I don't think that's the case. I think she's someone who wants closure. Her family is all gone."

"We can't just add a new person to our family! She might be your daughter—"

"Emphasis on *might*."

"*Might* be your daughter. But she's a stranger. How's that going to work? I'm thinking about the boys as well as you and me."

"I have no idea. But she lives thousands of miles away. It's not like she's planning to move into the spare room."

"Or so you believe." She folded her arms across her chest. "I suppose I should meet her. Then we need to talk to the boys."

MARTY CALLED RACHAEL EISEN that afternoon and set up a repeat visit at Coffee Diva. They met the next morning. "Thank you for coming!" Rachael said after Marty introduced her to his wife. "I'm sure this is … a little unsettling. I'm sorry for that."

"Yes, it's a bit of a surprise."

Carole was wary and tense. Marty had hoped she wouldn't be, but what could he have expected? He'd had a few days to get used to the idea of a daughter. His wife had had less than 24 hours.

They chatted about Rachael's work, carefully avoiding any talk of a DNA test or of Marty's relationship with Rachael's mother. After an hour, Carole was loosening up. When conversation dwindled, Carole stood up and said, "We need to get home. It was very interesting to meet you, Rachael."

Marty and Rachael stood. Marty wondered what to say next, what their next step should be.

"We need to talk to our children," Carole said, as if she'd read Marty's mind. "Before doing anything else."

"Of course," Rachael said.

"They're coming over for dinner tonight."

"You have my number," Rachael said to Marty.

Marty nodded.

On the drive home, Marty said, "I didn't know the boys were coming over for dinner."

"They are now," Carole said.

THE "BOYS" WERE JEFFERY AND Tanner. Jeffery, thirty-one, worked as a software engineer at Microsoft; his wife, Anne, was six months pregnant with their first child. Tanner was four years younger and single; he was a graphic designer at Amazon.

Before dinner Marty made jokes, asked the boys about their jobs, talked to Anne about her pregnancy, and carefully avoided any mention of the reason they'd been summoned.

By the time the main course was being passed around, Carole had obviously tired of waiting for him. "Your father has something he'd like to tell you," she said.

All eyes went to Marty. "Yeah, Dad, what's up?" Tanner asked. "Why the sudden dinner invitation?"

"You're not having a health problem, are you?" Jeffery said.

"Well … I … we … no, not a health problem … I …"

"You might have a sister," Carole said.

"You're not …" Both boys looked at their mother with shocked faces.

"Don't be ridiculous!" she said. "I'm fifty-seven years old."

"A grown sister," Marty said. "Older than either of you."

"Really?" Jeffery said. His eyes bounced between Marty and Carole.

"Mine, not your mother's," Marty said. "I may have gotten my high school girlfriend pregnant. She left for a foreign country just after we broke up. Six months later she had a child."

"High school? You were … In high school?" Tanner said.

"After all those lectures you gave us about teenage sex?" Jeffery added.

Tanner made his voice deep and admonitory. "You need to learn how to form a lasting relationship. Learn that first and worry about sex later." He shook his head and resumed his normal tone. "And you were doing it in high school?"

"Those lectures still stand. Did you ever think they might have been based on my personal experience?"

Their faces showed that no, it had never occurred to them that their father had had sex in high school, or maybe any sexual thoughts at all, ever.

"Besides," Marty added, "she got pregnant … if I had anything to do with it … which I may not have … when we were in college. We were almost twenty."

"Oh, well," Tanner said in a mocking tone. "As long as you were almost twenty …"

"What do you mean, 'if you had anything to do with it'?" Jeffery asked.

"It's possible the child … well, she's a middle-aged woman now … isn't mine."

"You mean she was sleeping around?" Tanner said.

"Not that I know of."

"She has your father's eyes," Carole said. "She's probably his."

"Are you going to do a DNA test?" Jeffery asked.

"That's what we need to talk to you about. How would you feel about a sister?"

Jeffery and Tanner looked at each other. Clearly they had no idea how they felt about a sister.

"Of course you have to think about it. We … I just sprang it on you. She lives thousands of miles away. You'd probably see her only rarely, if ever."

"Who is she?" Jeffery asked.

"We're not saying," Carole said, "until there's conclusive proof. But your father and I have met her. She seems nice. I liked her a lot."

That was news to Marty; Carole had kept her reactions to herself. "She's a journalist," Marty added. "Quite well known, although I'd never heard of her. An expert in her field. She's a very accomplished person."

"Is her mother still living?" Anne, Jeffery's wife, said thoughtfully. Until now she'd kept out of the discussion.

"No," Marty said. "She has no family left at all. Except possibly us."

"I think you should do it." Anne said. " Family is important."

MARTY CALLED RACHAEL EISEN the next morning. They met at her hotel room and used cotton swabs to take samples for the DNA test, then mailed them to a lab.

That evening, Marty, Carole, and Rachael met at Chinook's, a seafood restaurant overlooking Fisherman's Terminal on Salmon Bay. Marty had reserved a comfortable table with good views of the commercial fishing boats, both small and large.

Conversation flowed freely, mostly focused on Tanner and Jeffery and the coming grandchild. When dinner was over, they headed for the door. Before going out, Rachael said she had to leave for Israel the next morning, before the DNA results would come back. "Thank you so much," she added. "You've been kind and understanding beyond anything I had a right to expect." Her eyes were moist. "I hope …" She took a deep breath. "I hope we really are family."

Marty opened his arms and gave her a long hug. When he was done, Carole gave her one too. They watched silently as she went to her car and drove off. Neither of them spoke much on the way home.

MARTY AND CAROLE HAD BEEN reading Rachael's blog on Mideast affairs, as well as past articles. Marty also regularly visited some of the more thoughtful online news sites. He felt better informed, although he had no idea what to do with the new information. "It's been weeks since the President called me and asked my advice," he joked to Carole.

Occasionally they speculated on the DNA report. "I'm convinced she's your daughter," Carole said. "She's got your eyes."

"You're probably right," Marty said. "I like her, and I admire her. I'd be proud to be her father. But what if I'm not? How would I feel about that? I didn't think I'd ever say this, but I'd be disappointed if she wasn't my daughter. More to the point, how would she feel about it? It seems to mean so much to her. She's counting on it. And if I'm not her father, then what? She has no other leads to follow."

WHEN THE DNA REPORT ARRIVED in the mail, Carole placed the envelope on the kitchen counter, in the place she always put Marty's correspondence. When Marty came home from work, he saw it there, on top; he recognized the lab's logo on the envelope.

The envelope stayed on top for three more days. Each afternoon Carole brought in the mail and moved the envelope to the top of Marty's pile. And each day Marty sorted through all his other mail and left the lab report alone. "I just want to be in the right frame of mind," he told Carole. Also, he'd stopped reading her blog and the news. "It reminds me of her," he said. "Be patient. I'm almost ready."

By Friday he felt he could face it. He came home from work and brewed himself a cup of tea and went onto the patio with the envelope. The evening was cool, so he built a fire in the outdoor fireplace—to make himself cozy and comfortable. He put the lab report on the table in front of the fire. Still, he didn't open the envelope. After a few minutes, he went back inside to his computer to check his email and the news reports.

When he went to Rachael's blog, there was a new entry. It was from the Committee for the Protection of Journalists. The entry said, in essence, that there would be no more posts. Rachael had been killed while researching a story in old Jerusalem. The CPJ was investigating.

Marty stared at the screen, reading and rereading the entry, hoping he'd gotten it wrong. He went to the Reuters website and found a small article under the heading "Correspondent Dies in Jerusalem." The *Christian Science Monitor* had a similar piece.

He left the computer, stunned. He walked numbly back to the patio and sat in the chair facing the fire, staring at the envelope.

TWENTY MINUTES LATER, MARTY heard his wife walking about the house. Her steps paused, evidently near his computer. Then he heard her gasp and say, "Oh no! Oh my God!" She called his name. He did not reply. Quick steps sounded in the hall as she looked for him. Still he did not reply. After a few minutes, she came out on the patio and sat quietly in the chair next to him. She'd been crying.

"You read about her?" she said.

He nodded.

"I'm so, so sorry," Carole said. "Were there any details?"

"Two sources, both saying the same thing. Apparently she was investigating the destruction of a home in east Jerusalem, in a section occupied mostly by Arabs. Some children started throwing rocks at Israeli soldiers. The soldiers ordered them to leave, then fired some shots. The children fled except for the youngest, a boy about ten years old who seemed too terrified to move." He sighed. "She went to the child—whether to comfort him, protect him, or tell him to leave, no one knows. Another shot was fired, and she was hit. It's not clear who did the shooting. The truth may never be known."

Carole nodded slowly. "She was a caring person."

"Yes. Compared to her, I'm ..." he waited while the tightness in his throat eased enough for him to talk. "I'm a smug, self-satisfied, self-centered bastard."

"You're a kind and gentle man," Carole said softly, "who's being much too hard on himself." She put her arm around his shoulder. "Was she your daughter?" Carole said.

"Don't know."

"The report was inconclusive?"

Marty picked up the poker and stirred something in the fire. Smoldering papers, still in the envelope, flamed. "Didn't read the report," Marty said.

He felt her arm stiffen on his shoulder, sensed her shocked gaze into the fire.

"She has ... had ... your eyes," Carole said at last.

"Yes, she had my eyes. But she didn't get her vision from me. Thank God for that! I gave her nothing. Not her courage, her compassion, her view of the world. Her mother and I had a romp, without a thought for the future or anything beyond our own pleasure and gratification."

Marty stirred the fire again. The ashes glowed. "Do you know what DNA stands for?" he said. "Do Not Ask. It stands for Do. Not. Ask. Like the poem: 'Do not ask. For whom the bell tolls.' If she really was my daughter, would I admire her any more? And if not, would my grief be any less?" A deep breath. "And do I really want to know that about myself?"

Marty tipped his head against Carole's shoulder and wept softly. In his heart he knew that he would never be comfortable again.

Reunion

June 14, 3:17 a.m. Four Seasons Hotel, Seattle

DANIEL BURDETT LAY AWAKE wondering: What was he going to do with the twenty-nine million dollars? Why did he break Jason Bentley's nose? And who was the naked lady sleeping so sweetly next to him in the king-size bed?

He sat up and propped a pillow behind his back. As was his habit, Daniel probed for the larger issues, the questions behind the questions. In this case they came down to: What is the purpose of life? Why is there evil in the world? And where does love come from?

People had pondered those questions since they sat in caves, gnawing on the bones of a woolly mammoth, and he was unlikely to arrive at better conclusions than they had. So he tried to break it down, like a complicated computer program or a mathematical problem—narrow the scope, eliminate a few variables, try a test case.

He started with the third question: Who was the naked lady

lying next to him? Wrong question. He knew who she *was*. She *was* Amy Collins. Twenty years ago, when he was seventeen, she *was* the love of his life. But because he'd been a late bloomer in the romance department (her too), he'd never gone further than putting his arm around her while watching a French movie, one with subtitles. Until eight hours ago he hadn't seen her since the senior prom.

So she *was* his high school girlfriend. But who would she be when she woke up?

Eight Hours Earlier. Sand Point Country Club, Seattle

"OKAY," SAID JIMMY SODERBERG, former student body president and emcee for the night's festivities, "who remembers the All-City Championship game?"

The crowd—reunioners from Theodore Roosevelt High School—cheered and clapped. Index fingers poked the air, proclaiming the Roughriders' victory on a gray November day twenty years ago. Daniel clapped his hands so lightly they made no noise. No one noticed his unenthusiasm because he sat alone at a small table, a glass of water in front of him.

"Stand up, Roger!" said Soderberg, in his deep, slow, easily mocked voice.

Roger Foxman was already standing—near the bar, surrounded by fawning classmates who were buying him drinks and telling him their favorite jokes. Foxman made a football-throwing motion with his right arm. More cheers from the crowd. On the second play of the big game, Foxman, the Roughriders' quarterback, unleashed a long pass; the tight end snagged it on the 40 and ran for a touchdown and the beginning of a 34-7 blowout. The reunion crowd went wild with the happy memory of it all.

Daniel, however, remembered when he was an undersized freshman, stuffed into a locker by Foxman. Foxman padlocked the door, leaving Daniel to yell and pound while other boys laughed at his distress. It was a two-hour claustrophobic ordeal that was ended by a janitor with a bolt cutter. To Daniel, high school had been a reverse purgatory, a place where evildoers like Foxman received unjust rewards while the virtuous were punished.

"And who got the most varsity letters?" Jimmy Soderberg now asked.

Various names were shouted, none of them Daniel's, whose parents had doomed him to athletic oblivion when he started kindergarten. He was born a week before the cut-off date for school enrollment, and his parents figured (correctly) that he was a bright kid who was ready to learn. Unfortunately that made him a year behind most of his classmates—not intellectually but physically. The early start, combined with poor eyesight and a slight build, meant he would never excel at team sports, or even be average.

"That's right!" Soderberg said. "Jake Coomes! Two varsity letters in football, two in basketball, and three in track! Stand up Jake!" The reunioners applauded; Daniel moved his hands but made no noise.

At the start of ninth grade, Daniel lagged behind in more than just athletics. One day in PE class, during shower time, Coomes, the future star athlete, made two rude comments about Daniel's dormant masculinity. Within a few months Coomes' epithets were no longer apt; nonetheless Daniel heard himself called "Twinkie" and "Garbanzos" for the rest of the year—and beyond.

Daniel rose and roamed the room with his glass of water in his hand while Jimmy Soderberg droned on. Back in a dark corner, he finally found the table he'd been searching for. He sat down across from its sole occupant. "Hey," he said.

"Hey yourself," Amy Collins replied, not looking up. Her index finger swiped across an iPhone, engaged in a game of Angry Birds. She lost the game and grimaced.

"I don't mean to intrude," Daniel said, "but to win that level you shouldn't use the green bird as a boomerang."

"Huh. I'll try that." She began a new game, still not looking his way.

"Otherwise you'll lose and get the smirking pig."

She motioned with her head to a place across the room. "Speaking of smirking pigs," she said.

Daniel looked where she had indicated and saw Brian Connelly and Jason Bentley in a corner, telling each other snarky jokes, just as they had in high school. "The ultimate smirking pigs," Daniel said. "You can use the boomerang bird on them anytime. When will those two grow up?"

"When palm trees grow at the North Pole." She faced him for the first time. "I never really thanked you for defending my honor, such as it was. Thanks."

One evening near the end of their junior year, Daniel had been manning the cash box for a computer club fundraiser. Connelly and Bentley, fresh from the gym's weight room, wandered by and hung out near Daniel, playing Hot-or-Not every time a girl walked into the auditorium. Amy Collins went through the door. Amy was short and trim, but had a pretty, round face and luscious, wavy hair. Bentley said "Hot." Connelly said "Not." The two started to argue, speculating in lurid detail on various aspects of Amy's body. Daniel first seethed, then exploded. "You know what would look good in *your* mouth?" he said. Bentley turned toward him, and Daniel hit him. It was the last thing Bentley expected. It surprised Daniel even more. Blood spewed from Bentley's broken nose and spattered his shirt. Daniel thought he'd be pounded to pudding, but Bentley staggered off—to Daniel's amazement he was actually *crying*—with Connelly behind and looking fearfully back at Daniel.

"I didn't think anyone else knew about that," Daniel said to

Amy, staring into his water glass. "You were already in the auditorium."

"Trina was behind the door, inside. She heard the whole thing and told me about it. Apparently you packed quite a wallop. Probably your greatest sports achievement."

"Actually, I was aiming for his teeth and hit his nose instead. And I'll bet Trina didn't see me reach into the cash drawer and wrap my fist around a roll of quarters before I hit him."

Amy nodded. "See? You really can learn something useful in a high school physics class."

"$F = MA$."

"Conservation of momentum."

The room was warm, and Amy fanned her face with a menu.

"Oppressive in here." Daniel said.

"Yeah. Hot, too. Have you seen BJ or Trina?"

"No sign," he said. "Have you seen Tucker, Phillip, or any of the other guys?"

She shook her head.

By his junior year Daniel had scraped together a small circle of like-minded boys who excelled at academics—and little else. As upperclassmen they were old enough to commandeer their own table for lunch. They talked about computers and science fiction movies and voiced serious—though (he knew now) largely superficial—comments about politics and world affairs. Most of all, his little clique made ironic jokes about classmates to whom they felt intellectually superior. The jocks and cheerleaders, the extroverts and party people, the beauty queens and studs—all got withering put-downs from Daniel and his cohorts. Of course, their targets never heard any of it face-to-face.

Like Daniel, Amy had gathered a circle of brainy introverts. At lunch, they sat at the table behind Daniel's. Despite a natural affinity, the two tables never mingled. Except for Daniel and Amy. For much of their senior year they went to movies together, sometimes followed by pizza. They even attended the senior prom as each other's date. Immediately after the prom she'd gone to visit relatives on the east coast, then started college at Wellesley. They didn't write or call each other. This was the first time he'd seen her since the prom.

"I guess I'm not surprised that none of our old gang showed up," Daniel said. "At least we have each other," he added in a sardonic tone. The banter had been the way they'd talked in high school; it startled Daniel to see how fast he'd reverted to old patterns.

"That's probably the sweetest thing anyone's going to say to me tonight," Amy replied, equally sardonic. Then she surprised him; she reached across the table and touched his hand, looking him in the eye. "It's nice to see you," she said, suddenly dropping the old tone. "Thank you for coming."

"Okay," said Jimmy Soderberg, "Who's been married the most times?" There were whoops and ooooohs from the reunioners. "Twice? Who's on their second marriage?" A few dozen hands went up. "Do I hear three? Who's on their third?"

All hands went down. "I hear Candy Swigert is on her fourth," Amy said quietly.

"That's not surprising."

"Yup," said Amy. "And quite a few in between." In high school, Candy was famously easy, a girl who would flop on the first date if she liked the looks of the guy.

"Who's got the most children?" Soderberg asked next. "Hold up a finger for each kid. Use both hands if you need to." He laughed and added, "Anyone need to take off their shoes and use their toes, too?" A few names were thrown out in jest.

Amy imitated Soderberg's voice. "How many out there have written three books on esoteric computer subjects? Oh, Daniel, I see your hand is up."

Daniel continued in the same style. "How many got an MBA at Stanford and became Chief Financial Officer at a high-tech startup? Amy, shouldn't you raise your hand?"

"How many created nine best-selling iPhone apps and sold their company last year for ninety million dollars?" she said, again mocking Jimmy Soderberg.

"I didn't get it all," Daniel said, using his normal voice. "Investors got forty percent of it."

"Still, not bad. Success is the best revenge."

"My wife didn't see me for three years, so she left. Took the two kids, the house, and half my shares in the company. Took the golden retriever, too. She and the investors wanted to cash out. After the divorce, she and the investors outvoted me, and the company was sold. So now I'm pushing forty with no job and no family except on alternate weekends—not even a dog to walk in the park. Is that success?"

"I'm sorry about your marriage." She cocked her head and gave him a quizzical look. "I read the press. You stayed for a year under the new owners, hit your target, and earned a fat bonus. So you ended up with …" Her eyes closed while she ran the numbers in her head, "about twenty-nine million dollars, including the bonus. That should keep you in donuts."

"In Silicon Valley, that's chump change. I would have done a lot better if they'd waited three more years."

"Aaaaah. Only twenty-nine million. Poor baby."

"I see I'm not going to get any sympathy."

"For the marriage, yes. I know how tough that is."

"Your marriage?"

"An unfortunate memory of the past."

"Like high school."

"You got it."

"How did Med-Rec work out?" Med-Rec was the Oregon-based start-up where Amy had been CFO.

"Well, the company failed. So … But financially, it was good for me … and horrible for almost everyone else. I negotiated a more conservative pre-IPO deal than the other execs. I took a lot of heat for it. 'Our CFO is an idiot.' Stuff like that. But I could sell my stock before they could. I cashed out when the company was still a Wall Street darling, then parked my money in muni bonds that were near maturity. When Med-Rec crashed and burned—along with the rest of Wall Street—I sold the bonds and bought quality stocks at bargain-basement prices. They went up when people figured out that Western civilization might stagger on for a few more years. It worked out well for me. Not as well as for you, but ... close."

Daniel nodded approval. "I'm happy for you."

Amy shrugged. "Money isn't everything. But it's very convenient sometimes."

"So what are you doing now?"

"Some consulting," Amy said, "but nothing full time. I'm enjoying the freedom. You?"

"Considering my options, as they say. I keep up on the technology trends—which takes a lot of time—but I don't know what I'll do next. I bought waterfront on Bainbridge Island, on Manzanita Bay. I spend most of my time there. I keep a condo in Santa Clara; I fly down every other weekend to see my kids."

"It's hard, isn't it? A couple of decades of push-push-push, then suddenly there's nothing."

"Yes. I get ... restless. Not knowing what's coming next. I bicycle a lot. Bainbridge is great; it has good hills."

Amy showed increased interest. "You're a cyclist now?" Her eyes narrowed. "What's your ride?"

They fell into a highly technical discussion of carbon frames, shifters, forks, brakes, and handlebar geometry. This was followed by lists of favorite rides, training regimens, and the problems of staying fit during the rainy Northwest winters. An enthusiastic discussion of electrolytes was interrupted by Jimmy Soderberg loudly asking, "Who can still fit into their prom dress?"

A few hands went up.

"Angela Pomeroy might if she hadn't gotten those ridiculous implants," Amy said quietly.

"Where'd she buy those things?" Daniel said. "Blue Light Special at Kmart?"

"More like a *Red* Light Special."

"I notice a lot of guys hanging around her table, so I guess she got what she wanted." He shook his head. "You should raise your hand. You'd fit into your prom dress. I loved that dress."

Amy raised her eyebrows. "You're nice," she said. "But apparently you forgot your glasses."

"I wear contacts now. And there's nothing wrong with them. Now where's that menu?" He pretended to fumble around the table like he was blind, finally picking up the menu. "Ah, here we are," he said, holding the menu upside down.

"Okay, who's still driving the same car they had in high school?" Jimmy Soderberg asked.

"Okay, who's been through rehab the most times?" Daniel said, imitating Jimmy Soderberg again. "Once? Michael Earnshaw, shouldn't your hand be up? Who's been through rehab twice?" He pretended to scan the room again. His eyes came back to Amy, who'd partially raised her hand and was looking at him sideways. He could see she was serious. "Oh my God!" he said, totally embarrassed at his flippancy. "I'm so sorry. Forgive me. I had no idea. You never touched anything in high school."

"My husband—ex-husband. He got me started. Said it would loosen me up for social functions. Problem was, I didn't know how to stop. Neither did he. After my second rehab, I divorced him. He told me I should drink with him, but I needed to learn to hold my liquor better. What I needed was to stay away from heavy drinkers. Like him and all his friends. So we split. No kids, fortunately." She swirled the 7Up in her glass. "I've been sober for eight years and two months. I still go to AA meetings."

"I'm sorry."

"Did you ever learn to drink?" She pointed to his glass of water.

"So many people tried to get me to take a beer that I rebelled, got stubborn. Besides, I couldn't stand the taste of the stuff. Yuk. Hard liquor's worse. I have a little wine now and then, but ... I don't like to lose control of my thinking. Not drinking became a habit. I was a *work*aholic instead." He looked away from her. The confession of her alcoholism had stunned him and seemed to call for reciprocal candor. "I worked so hard my wife ... found someone else."

She touched his hand again. "I'm so sorry," she said sincerely. "That had to be hard." She stood up and said, "How about a walk?" He rose, and she linked her arm in his as they left the clubhouse with its crowd of boisterous reunioners. The golf course was nearly deserted and reflected the golden light of the setting sun. They picked up the cart path and followed it.

"I chatted with the caterer," Amy said as they walked. "There was another Roosevelt reunion here last night. A fortieth."

"Forty years? Imagine! Do you think by that time all the high school BS has faded away and people can just be themselves?"

"That would be cool, wouldn't it! To be pushing sixty instead of forty, looking forward to a quiet retirement, everything from your youth is a distant memory and not going to come back and haunt you. Almost makes you envious of old people!"

"Almost. But not quite!"

They walked and talked until they reached the ninth green; then they followed the back nine toward the clubhouse. They were alone, and darkness was settling in. The darker it got, the more relaxed Daniel became. Conversation was easy and natural; the ironic banter had faded away. Daniel remembered why he'd liked her so much.

"Too bad our friends didn't come," he said.

Amy shrugged. "I'm glad I came." She faced him. "Because you're here."

"I'll tell you a secret," Daniel said hesitantly. "The real reason I came … I hoped you might be here. I wanted to see you again, find out how you're doing."

Amy kicked a fir cone out of the path. "Where are you staying?"

"I'll just take the ferry back to Bainbridge. You?"

"I drove up from Oregon this morning. I'm staying downtown. At the Four Seasons."

They were silent for a while. The sun was long gone. They were cloaked in darkness, like they were the only people on earth.

"How come we weren't more serious when we were in high school?" Amy said quietly.

"I thought we *were* serious. We did things together for most of the year. I never went out with anyone else."

"Me neither. But you know what I mean."

Daniel nodded. "I know." He thought carefully before speaking next. "I was very fond of you."

"And I of you."

He wasn't sure he should say more, but he took the risk. "I was more than fond. I adored you. I'd never felt that way about anyone before. I'm … not sure I have since."

She looked hard at him, then turned away. "I can say the same. I loved you very much. I thought about you constantly."

Daniel looked straight ahead, not at her. "And I loved you."

"Can people be in love if neither of them admits it to the other?" Amy asked. "If there's no mutual declaration? No … expression … of any kind?"

"I don't know."

An intimate silence hung between them as they walked on; then Amy said, "I thought you might be gay. And that's why you never tried to even kiss me."

He stared at her, barely perceptible in the darkness. "Really? You wondered about my sexuality?"

"Or maybe some sort of … you know … developmental problem. There were those … nicknames." She paused. "Twinkie," she said with a sly, slightly embarrassed smile. "Garbanzos," she added, speaking out the side of her mouth.

"That bastard Coomes! I think I'll find out what company he works for, buy it, and fire him in the most public and humiliating way I can think of."

"He's at Boeing. "

"Damn! I don't think I have that much money!"

"You're not, are you?"

"Gay? Not now, not then. Don't plan on changing." He bit his lip and got serious. "It wasn't like I didn't want to … to kiss you."

"What stopped you?"

"Fear of rejection."

"You wouldn't have been rejected."

"I didn't know that."

"And I didn't know how to encourage a guy or give the right signs."

"You could have given me all the signs in the world, and I wouldn't have known how to read them. Or would still have had my doubts. Trust me, I dreamed about kissing you."

"Likewise."

They stopped walking and faced each other. The darkness was total, but they were almost in range of the clubhouse's bright lights. They stood in the shelter of a tall fir tree, hidden in a world of their own. Amy laced her fingers in his and pulled him close. "Do it now," she whispered. "Like you dreamed about doing it." She tipped her head and closed her eyes.

Did she really mean it? Or was she just being ironic? Was he misreading the signs? And why did he feel like he was seventeen again? Tentatively, Daniel leaned into her and kissed her on the lips, briefly.

"That's it?" she said, her eyes now open. "That's what you dreamed about? I thought you had more imagination than that. More

… *garbanzos*." She tipped her head again. Her eyes closed, expectantly.

Apparently, Daniel thought, Amy had learned a thing or two about how to encourage a guy and give him clear signs. He put his right arm around her waist, pulled her close, and kissed her with more feeling. She kissed him back with equal fervor.

The intensity of their embrace increased more and more. After two minutes their loins were pressed so closely together that there was no way she could not have detected his growing arousal. They'd gone far past any point he'd imagined when they were teenagers.

Finally she pulled back, breathing hard. "That's more like it," she said. Even in the darkness he could see that her cheeks were flushed. "I knew you had it in you." She disengaged completely. "Got your cell phone?"

He nodded, confused. This was not the sort of love-talk he'd expected.

"What's your number?"

He gave her the number, which she poked into her contact list. "I'm going to the Ladies," she said abruptly, and left.

Daniel stood by himself, wondering what the hell had just happened and if she was coming back or what. His phone vibrated. He read the text: "Four Seasons. Room 617. Leave now."

He stared at his phone for at least a minute before he poked "c u soon" into the reply line. He stood with his finger poised, thinking. Finally, he pushed the Send button.

SO HE'D COME TO HER ROOM, and they'd made love. And now he wondered what it meant and who she was. No: who she *is*.

While he thought, his eyes adjusted to the darkness. He could make out the vague shapes and shadows of the hotel room, which was spacious but not ostentatious. The furnishings were modern and, like many things in Seattle, Asian-influenced without being actually

Asian. The drapes were open to a view of Puget Sound, although there was little to see in the early morning dimness. A few lights shone in nearby buildings. He could hear an occasional car in the street below.

Amy stirred, then propped herself on one elbow, looking at him through half-closed eyes.

"Nice room," Daniel said.

"I don't normally do this," she said.

"Invite old boy friends to your room?"

"Stay at the Four Seasons. I'm a Holiday Inn kind of girl—rather save the money. Also ... I'm not in the habit of inviting men to my room, wherever I stay."

"How come you did it this time?"

"Stay at the Four Seasons or invite you to my room?"

"Both."

"I was unsure about the reunion, about seeing all those people again. I figured my gang wouldn't come, but I thought you might. So I got the nice room ... as a treat, an indulgence ... in case you weren't there."

"And me?"

She hesitated. "As I said, I don't do this sort of thing on a regular basis. Like ... never before. It was spur of the moment. I felt so connected, like old times. And there were ... unrequited longings ... regrets for steps not taken ... wondering what might have been. Anyway, I'm glad you came. Very passionate! Not bad for two people who dated for most of a year but couldn't get up the courage to hold hands. Of course I had to text the invitation to you; some of the old shyness is still there."

He nodded. "I think that's sweet and old fashioned, in a high-tech sort of way. But what would you have done if I hadn't come?"

"I'd have gone back to my nice room, flopped on the bed, and had a good cry. Then I'd have ordered a triple banana split from room service and eaten it while soaking in that big tub in the bathroom."

"Good thing I came, then. Those banana splits are terribly caloric."

"And I never know how much to tip the guy who brings it."

"Yeah, tip-anxiety." He shuddered. "Who needs it?" He paused, suddenly serious. "I have a big question."

She looked at him tentatively. "Yes …"

"Why did I hit Jason Bentley and break his nose? You know, back then."

"Because you had bad aim and missed his teeth? Those thick glasses you wore probably had a lot of distortion. I don't know how you saw anything at all."

"That's why I switched to contacts."

"So you could punch people better?"

"Seriously … why did I slug Bentley?"

"Because he was a vile butthead who deserved it. Maybe you were God's avenging angel. That's how I thought of you."

"There are a lot of vile buttheads in the world, especially in high school. If I slugged every one of them, then I wouldn't be an avenging angel—I'd be the devil's own bully, as bad as them. Why him? Why then?"

She thought for a while, then said, "Well, not to sound egotistical, but … would you have hit him if he'd been talking about Trina or BJ?"

"Good point. I'd have gotten mad and disgusted, but I wouldn't have done anything. It was because he was talking about you."

"Maybe we had feelings for each other before we even dated, inklings we weren't fully aware of. I'd always respected and liked you—"

"And I'd respected and liked you."

"So maybe," she said, "there was a connection that we weren't conscious of. After you hit him, I noticed you a lot more, thought about you, wanted to know you better."

"Perhaps that was the beginning of all things."

"A path that led to—"

"Room 617 at the Four Seasons," Daniel said. "Maybe I should look up Bentley and thank him."

"For his vile buttheadedness."

They fell silent and thoughtful. After a few minutes he asked, "What am I going to do with my money?"

"Your vast millions?"

"That's part of the problem: it's not all that vast, at least in today's world. Like I said before, it's chump change down in Silicon Valley. It's not that much in Seattle, either; there's a lot of high-tech money floating around this town."

"Any debts? Do you have expensive tastes?"

"No debts. And my tastes aren't extravagant. I've got a nice car, modest waterfront on Bainbridge Island with a modest sailboat, and all the bicycles I need. I have state-of-the-art electronics and entertainment gear, but nothing outlandish. Going forward, I can't imagine spending more than twenty percent of my income. It's just piling up."

"Another start-up venture?"

"Been there and done that. I no longer feel the need to prove anything or impress anyone. Besides, the price—the personal price—is too high. I want a different kind of life than I've had." He looked away and sighed, not sure how much to say, then plunged ahead. "I was sleeping at the office—I had a small bedroom and shower for overnight stays during project crunches. I was getting three hours of sleep a night, at best. I came home and found my wife had moved out—two days before. I didn't even know it. I'm never going to let work take over my life like that again."

She touched his arm tenderly. "I know what you mean about work. The high-tech world can be so demanding and stressful. It can destroy a person. I don't want to go back to it, either. And, like you, I don't feel impelled to impress anybody anymore."

"So what are you going to do?"

She shrugged. "I've decided I don't need to know yet. Are you anxious? Worried about the future?"

"No, the future doesn't worry me. I've been dealing with the future all my life. As you know, that's what high tech is all about. But I realized something tonight at the reunion … I'm comfortable with the future, but the past scares the hell out of me."

"The past? But it's over and done with, never to be seen again!"

"Not as much as we'd like. For the first time, I saw that a lot of what I've achieved has been about seeing how far I could go. And part of that drive came from a lingering sense of inadequacy—old issues from my teens."

She chewed her lip, then asked, "What about tonight? Was this about the past?"

"The past. The present. And I hope the future."

TO THE SOUTH, DANIEL SAW A ferryboat leave the terminal, all bigness, bustle, and bright lights. He knew it was the 5:30 to Bainbridge Island, the first boat of the day. Sometime soon the sun would rise, this interlude would end, and he would board one of those ferries. But not yet. Sometime he'd know the answer to his biggest question—who was she? … no, who *is* she? … no, who *are we?* But not yet.

They made love again. Their first time had been rushed and intense—like their lives to date. But this time was tender and lingering, each caring more for pleasing the other. And in that tender, caring, making, pleasing, loving—he glimpsed a path to a future without a past, a future with better answers to all the right questions. And he wanted to explore that path with her.

Judd Faces Reality

August 23, Maupin

WHEN HE SAW THE WHITE Subaru Outback, Judd Boone's blood
ran cold— not because there had been an accident nor because
Subarus are scary automobiles, but because this Subaru belonged to
his daughter, Megan. And it was parked in front of the house of Casey
Williams. And it was two o'clock in the morning, and the house was
dark.

Judd knew it was Megan's car; he had helped her pick it out,
had recommended a white one for visibility and better resale. He
knew the license plate. And he knew that Megan and Casey were
seeing each other. What he hadn't known was that their relationship
had become serious—and by "serious" he meant sexual, although he
wouldn't use the word, even to himself.

Judd had driven to Idaho to pick up a new-used driftboat for
his guiding business. His intent had been to stay overnight in Boise.

But Judd didn't like motels, even though he owned one, and he'd headed for home despite the long drive and late hour. He'd hoped to surprise his family. Instead, he was the surprised one.

WHEN HE AROSE THE NEXT morning, Judd decided he was mistaken about Casey and his daughter. No doubt her car had developed some sort of mechanical problem, and Casey was fixing it for her. Judd decided that a nice guy like that deserves a helping hand, so he skipped breakfast and drove up the hill to Casey's, arriving about 7:15.

He expected—hoped?—Megan's car would be parked in front, hood up, Casey leaning over the fender tinkering with something. But Megan's car was gone. Casey's truck and driftboat were absent, too. Then Judd remembered that the young man was guiding two couples on a four-day float trip from Beavertail to the mouth of the Deschutes. He also remembered that Casey didn't know a thing about fixing cars. And besides, who can do their own work on cars anymore, they're so damned complicated?

As he drove back to the OK Cafe, his stomach was nervous and unsettled—lack of breakfast, he figured. Solid food didn't sound good, though. Maybe a nice hot cup of something would help; he'd go into the OK and get one of those latte things from that fancy new machine they'd installed back in May.

Judd slid into a booth, latte in hand. While sipping the foam off his drink, he thought about the situation. Casey was nearly thirty and Megan a year younger. For the last seven years, Megan had taught high school English in Portland. She'd lived with Jeff, her college boyfriend, the first year. Then she'd lived alone for four years before moving in with Curt, a software designer. This spring she'd split with Curt and moved back to Maupin, getting her own place to live and teaching in the local school.

So why should he be bothered that Casey and Megan were

"serious"? *If* they were serious, he reminded himself. The sticking point, he had to admit, was this: Casey worked for Judd, and in reality was more than an employee. When the young man was a troubled seventeen-year-old, Judd stepped in and helped Casey turn his life around. During their senior year of high school, Casey and Megan had developed an attachment. It looked like love, at least to Judd, but they broke up during Megan's freshman year of college—why, Judd didn't know. The one thing he was certain about, however, was that Casey and Megan's earlier relationship was not serious.

So Casey was a kind of surrogate son, as well as Judd's head fly fishing guide. In reality, of course, Judd owned the Rainbow Anglers Guide Service, as well as the OK Cafe and Resort, so *he* was the head guide. And there were only two guides who worked for him—one of whom was part time—plus Willie, who rowed the bag boat. But still, he called Casey his "head guide" because it sounded good. Judd was fond of the kid and proud of how he had matured, even though he still had some rough edges. But … Casey and Megan?

Judd was halfway through his latte when Megan entered the OK, smiling and humming a cheerful tune. She looked radiant. Maybe she'd just heard her favorite song on the car radio.

Megan ordered a latte of her own, then looked for a place to sit down. That's when she saw Judd. "Oh! Dad!" she said. "I didn't know you were home." She sat down opposite him. "I thought you wouldn't be back until this afternoon."

"Finished up early and made the push for home last night."

"So what time … did you … get in?" Megan asked. She wouldn't look at him.

"About two."

"Um … two. In the morning." She licked her lips. "That's early. Or late, depending on how you look at it." She glanced at him, then pointed tentatively at her upper lip. "Foam," she said.

"Huh? Oh, right." Judd picked up a napkin and wiped the latte foam from his mouth. "Still not used to these things."

A silence followed; then Megan asked, "What … um … what route did you take to get home? Did you come up from The Dalles or take 216 through Grass Valley?" The first route went by Casey's place; the other did not.

"You know," Judd said, "it was late, and I was so bleary-eyed that I don't remember." God, he hated lying. He sipped some more latte, trying not to get a foam moustache. "Shouldn't drive when I'm like that. Don't see things well."

"How … um … was your float from Trout Creek last week? I haven't talked to you since then. They were new clients, weren't they?"

"Yeah," Judd said, glad for the change of subject.

"Did you like them?"

"At first I didn't think so. They started all *Veni, vidi, kvetchy*—'I came, I saw, I bitched about it.' But after they woke up and caught some fish, they were fine. Nice tip."

"You have to remember that most people don't get up at four in the morning."

"Yeah, yeah. I only get up that early in summer. Winters, I sleep late. Six, sometimes seven, even. Summers are for working. Winters are for sleeping."

"Casey's on a four-day float. From Beavertail."

"Uh-huh. Yeah." He sipped some more latte. He was happier when they weren't talking about his head guide.

"Back on Thursday."

"Right."

"Four days from now."

"Yup."

"I hope they have good fishing."

"Uh-huh."

They finished their lattes in silence, looking at the table, out the window, into the kitchen, and anywhere that wasn't each other's eyes.

HE SAW HIS DAUGHTER ON and off over the next few days. Their conversations continued to be stilted, but he noticed that Megan's glow increased as the day of Casey's return approached. He'd concluded that it wouldn't be a bad thing if they had a serious relationship. Still, he figured he'd be at the OK Friday morning. He knew that Casey and Megan had a routine of meeting around 8:00 and having an espresso drink together on days he wasn't guiding. Megan always got a two-shot twelve-ounce latte, while Casey was fond of sixteen-ounce mochas.

When Judd arrived Friday morning, Megan was already sitting at her usual table. She had a smile of anticipation. Well, what of it. Young love! What a wonderful thing! He was glad for them. Who was he to sit in judgment over two consenting adults? So what if one was his daughter and the other his head guide? Casey was a good man, and he couldn't wish Megan any better. When Casey came in for his mocha, Judd would greet him warmly. But not too warmly. Just enough to let the young man know that he liked him. But not so much as to let on that he knew what was going on between him and his daughter. Just enough to let Megan know that he approved. But not enough to reveal that he'd seen her Subaru at Casey's at two in the morning.

Megan asked, "Did you hear from Casey last night? I wondered how his trip went."

Judd shrugged. "Not a word." He wanted to know why his daughter didn't know the answer to her question. Maybe she and Casey were so busy making goo-goo eyes that she forgot to ask him last night. If they were serious, he'd have gone straight to her place when he got back from his trip, right? Or at least called her.

Half an hour passed, and Casey was a no-show. Megan's once-happy face now revealed other emotions: concern? disappointment? anger? She ordered a second latte and sipped it slowly. Still no Casey. After an hour and a half, Megan stood up, tight-lipped, and left without a word.

Judd wondered if he should follow her out the door, put his arm around her, and give some words of fatherly advice. Like what? "Hey, Sweetie, it's okay if you're serious with my head guide ..." Or maybe he'd just keep his mouth shut.

By noon, Judd felt irritable. By the end of the day he was really pissed. How dare Casey sleep with his daughter, then treat her so callously! Maybe he should go to Casey's house and tell that sonofabitch how to treat a woman. But he thought better of it and decided to talk to his wife.

"CASEY AND MEGAN ARE SEEING each other again," he said to Susan, his wife of thirty-five years, over dinner that night.

"Yes. I know," Susan said. "That's been going on for a while. Where have you been?"

"Well, I knew they were seeing each other. Again. Do you think they're serious?"

"Maybe."

"How serious do you think they are?"

She shrugged. "How serious do *you* think they are?"

He echoed her shrug; a shrug seemed less like lying. He took another bite of mashed potatoes, then said, "She's careful, right? Knows about ... you know ... safety stuff."

Susan put down her fork and looked at him in disbelief. "Your daughter is an educated and intelligent twenty-nine-year-old woman, and this is the twenty-first century. She's lived with two different guys. Have you seen any grandchildren running around?"

"I guess not."

"Did you think she and Jeff had a platonic relationship? That she shared a bedroom with Curt so she could save on the rent?"

"Well, no."

"She's known about these things since she was twelve." She turned away, eying him sideways. "No thanks to you, I might add."

"Okay, okay."

"Judd, Honey," she said gently, "you're an upfront and plain-spoken man. But I know it's hard for you to talk frankly about these things when it's your daughters."

Judd acknowledged her with a head shake.

"My father was the same way when you and I started dating. And got serious."

"Really?"

"That's how it is with fathers and daughters. Especially the youngest."

Judd finished his dinner in silence but stayed at the table, thinking. Louie, their large, tawny cat, jumped into his lap and sought attention. Judd scratched Louie in his favorite spots, then said, "I just can't help wondering when theory turned into practice."

His wife eyed him over the top of her glasses. "Do you really want to know the answer to that? What if it was longer ago than you think? Would that change how you feel about her? And about Casey? I intend to stay out of her love life. As I always have, unless I'm asked to get involved. I suggest you do the same."

That night, as he lay awake staring at the ceiling, Judd reflected on his conversation with Susan. What did she mean by *What if it was longer ago than you think?* And that final remark, *And about Casey?* The comment seemed to imply something more serious about their earlier relationship, something his wife knew about or suspected. For the first time, Judd began to think that Casey and his daughter may have been serious when she was nineteen. My God, she was a teenager! Well, barely. And it was ten years ago. Why should he be bothered now?

He also wondered about their breakup. There had been unexplained events, evasions, glib answers. What was that all about?

THE FOLLOWING MORNING Judd stood by the OK's grill

scrambling eggs and frying hash browns for customers. Helen, his married daughter, waited tables.

Judd heard a pickup truck enter the gravel parking lot. He turned to look. It was Casey, who took an outside table. Right behind him came Megan's Subaru. The sound of sizzling eggs made him return his attention to the grill, reluctantly. He pushed the eggs around, then looked outside again. Casey and Megan sat at a table. Judd couldn't hear what they were saying, but it had the appearance of tension and awkwardness. Casey looked sheepish; Megan looked mad. Then Megan stood up, shouted something, and stomped off.

"Dad!" said Helen. "Your eggs are burning!"

Judd looked down at the grill. "Damn!" He scrapped the eggs off and started over, looking furtively out the window. Megan had driven off, but Casey sat at the table looking stunned. Helen went out and said something to Casey, who then looked even more stunned. Then Helen came back in, scowling and angry.

"Anything wrong?" Judd asked her.

"Nothing!" Helen snapped.

Through the window, Judd could see Casey walking quickly down the street toward Dave Tindal's fly shop. Judd opened the door, ready to run after him. He could see Hank O'Leary's blue F-250 pickup in Dave's parking lot.

"Dad!" Helen called to him. "Mind those eggs!" Then, softer: "Are you okay?"

"Huh? Oh, right. I'm fine." He closed the door and returned to the grill.

THE NEXT DAY JUDD HAD TWO clients who wanted to fish for trout between Warm Springs and Trout Creek, a one-day trip. Despite the fact that August is one of the worst months for trout fishing, Judd found them some fish, and his clients felt satisfied enough to quit before sunset. They arrived at the Trout Creek boat ramp around 7:30.

As Judd winched his driftboat onto its trailer, Hank O'Leary backed his boat next to Judd's. Apparently Hank and his girlfriend were doing a multiday float to Maupin.

"Late start, Hank," Judd said when Hank got out of his truck.

"We're just going to Rainbow Camp tonight. We'll fish the evening caddis hatch, then push on in the morning."

Although Hank was Judd's age, Hank and Casey were friends in a way that Judd and Casey couldn't be. Casey probably told Hank things that he wouldn't tell Judd, especially if it involved Megan. "Seen Casey lately?" Judd asked.

"Off and on. Saw him yesterday at Dave Tindal's fly shop."

Judd already knew that, of course, but didn't mention it. "He's been seeing Megan again, you know."

"Yes. I know."

"Do you think they're serious?"

"I think you should ask them that question, not me." Hank loosened his boat's tiedown strap. "Or maybe you shouldn't ask the question at all."

"Does he talk to you about her?"

Hank turned from his boat and looked Judd in the eye, frowning. "Like I said …"

"How serious do you think they are?"

"Judd …"

"How serious do you think they were ten years ago?"

Hank took a deep breath and gave Judd a hard stare for the space of a slow exhale.

"Yeah, okay," Judd said. "I hear you. Or don't hear you. The silence is deafening."

Hank pursed his lips. "Judd, let me ask you something. When you were growing up, did you tell your mom and dad everything you got up to?"

"God no. They'd have killed me."

"Do you think your parents had a pretty good idea anyway?"

"I ... I suppose so."

"Why do you think nobody said anything?"

"Well, because ... I ... well ..."

"Do you think maybe it was better that way? Better if everybody knew, but nobody said?"

"Um ..." Judd waved Hank off. "Have a nice trip."

THAT NIGHT, SUSAN WAS AT A committee meeting for the upcoming RiverFest, so Judd took his dinner at the OK. He ate carefully, cutting his pork chop into small pieces and chewing thoughtfully. Halfway through his second chop, he resolved to face reality. Casey and his daughter had slept together. They'd probably slept together when she was nineteen. He was going to have to get used to the notion and not worry about it. Facts are facts. There's no denying them, and nothing you can do will make them go away.

He turned to Logan McCrea, sitting by the espresso machine and reading a book. "Isn't that right, Logan?" he said.

"Isn't what right?"

"We have to go eyeball to eyeball with the facts. We shouldn't delude ourselves. You're a man with a technical education—computers, science, all that stuff. That must give a guy objectivity, an ability to see things as they really are. To face reality."

"Well, yes. Face reality." He cocked his head and looked away from Judd. "Whatever reality is," he said, more to himself than to Judd.

"What do you mean, 'Whatever reality is'? You know what it is. All this!" Judd waved his fork—a piece of pork chop impaled on the tines—around the OK Cafe, then pointed it at Logan. "The physical world in front of our eyes! Reality! We have to see things as they are, not how we'd like them to be."

"All that 'stuff' in front of us," Logan said, "the atoms,

molecules, and physical world? It's called *baryonic matter.* There's also dark matter and dark energy. It's ninety six percent of what exists."

"Okay, so barry ... whatever ... matter is ninety-six percent, and then there's some leftovers called dark—"

"Other way around. Baryonic matter is about four percent of what exists. What we see ... " Logan swung his arm around the room "is a tiny fraction of creation. A side show. The vast majority of the universe consists of things we can't perceive and know nothing about."

"Know nothing about ... " Judd muttered. He had a sudden thought. "But all this dark matter and dark energy doesn't affect us. It's like a separate world that has nothing to do with our—"

"—with our little four percent?"

"Right. Nothing to do with us." Judd folded his arms across his chest, feeling more secure.

"Actually ... the dark matter and dark energy hold the universe together. Without it, everything falls to pieces."

Judd tried to puzzle this out. "So the only thing keeping the planets in their orbits, the stars and galaxies in their courses, and us from flying apart ... is stuff we know nothing about? Dark matter and dark energy are the glue that holds the universe together?"

"You got it." Here Logan paused, grimaced a bit, and said, "Uh ... Judd? I don't think you're going to like this but ... it's actually not a universe. It's a multiverse."

"Huh?"

"A multiverse. At least according to many of the top cosmologists. I'm just a computer wonk, not a physicist, but the way I understand it is like this." He paused and settled himself. "The classic thought experiment is Schroedinger's cat. Suppose there's a—"

"Is that the *Peanuts* kid? The one that plays the piano? I don't remember a cat."

"Schroedinger, not Schroeder. Suppose there's a cat in a shoe box." Logan paused again, then said, "I'm simplifying here, so bear with me. Anyway, the question is, is the cat alive or dead? Mathematically—"

"If there aren't any air holes in the box, the cat is dead. Or soon will be."

"Okay, there are air holes in the lid. Is the cat alive or dead? According to—"

"If there are air holes in the lid, you can see the cat through the holes. If it's moving, it's alive." Logan was starting to look impatient, so Judd said, "Go on. I'll keep quiet while you tell me about the cat in the box."

"According to physics ..." Logan looked at Judd like he half-expected another interruption. When Judd held his peace, Logan went on. "The cat is in a superposition of states, being both alive *and* dead, until the lid is removed. Only when you take off the lid does it become alive or dead—to you, the observer."

Judd tried to digest this. He'd had no idea that physicists were so interested in cats.

Logan continued. "That's the Copenhagen interpretation of quantum physics. In the Many Worlds interpretation, however, there is a live cat and an observer in one universe, and in another universe there is a dead cat and an observer. There are an infinite number of universes, each with different outcomes. A multiverse."

"Well, I wouldn't want to be the one to take the lid off," Judd said, "because one of those worlds is going to have a really pissed-off cat."

A FEW DAYS LATER, JUDD WAS in the OK when Hank O'Leary walked in with his girlfriend, Jackie. Jackie ordered a couple of lattes and stood by the espresso machine. Hank sidled next to Judd. They spoke quietly about the fishing trip Hank and Jackie had just finished;

then Hank said, "Sorry if I was a bit short with you at the boat ramp the other day."

"Don't worry, Hank. I should have left you out of it."

"Sounds like you found a measure of peace."

"I did." Judd pushed back his Stetson. "It's like this, Hank. The cat's in the box. You have to ask yourself, Do you want a live cat or a dead cat? Which one makes you happier? Sometimes it's better to leave the lid on the box and not know the answer."

"Judd, have you been drinking?"

"Sober as a judge! Depending on the judge, of course."

"Is the judge in the box with the cat?"

"Hank, I've learned that the stuff we don't know anything about—the dark stuff—is the glue that keeps everything together. Without it, the universe would fly into pieces. The cat might be alive or dead, and as long as I don't take the lid off the box, my little piece of the universe holds together."

THE NEXT DAY, JUDD WAS around the back of the OK getting his gear ready for a three-day guide trip, Macks Canyon to the mouth. He saw Megan and Casey come out with their drinks and sit at an outside table. They were both smiling and chatty, although out of earshot. He occasionally looked up from his work to see how they were doing. They seemed to be happy.

Judd felt something bump against his shin. It was Louie the cat. He reached down and rubbed the cat's back. Louie purred and begged to be picked up. Judd obliged him, and Louie closed his eyes and kneaded Judd's arm with his paws. "You're a happy cat," Judd said quietly to Louie. He scratched Louie behind the ears; Louie rubbed his head on Judd's hand. "Maybe you're so happy because you're not in a box," Judd added.

He glanced at his daughter and head guide. Casey said something, and Megan laughed—carefree and joyous. Casey said something more, and they laughed together. When Judd finished prepping his boat half an hour later, they were still there, still laughing, still enjoying each other's company.

Judd decided that was all the reality he needed to know. Anything more might cause the universe to fly apart.

The Pledge

October 8, Maupin

"ARE WE AGREED?" SAID REX Navarre. "No late nights, no drinking, no overeating or junk food. And no chasing women or even thinking about them! Up before dawn, fish until dark. Total focus on steelhead!" He looked around at his two sons and his nephew.

"No problem," said Dwayne, his firstborn.

"Whatever," said Lonnie, his sister's son.

"How am I supposed to not *think* about women for two weeks?" said Barry, Rex's youngest. "I'm a guy!"

Rex was not surprised. Barry—twenty-eight and in a solid career as a software engineer—loved women. Computers and girls had gotten ninety percent of his mental bandwidth since puberty.

"Well," said Rex, "not thinking about them might be too much to ask, especially for you. Just don't chase them. And try to focus on fishing."

"Okay, okay. But only for two weeks."

Rex put his hand on the table. "Swear," he said. Barry put his hand on top of his father's. Lonnie and Dwayne followed suit. With varying enthusiasm, the three young men said, "Resolved," in unison.

This act of resolution was an old family ritual, and Rex hoped his two sons and nephew would abide by it. He'd rented the house in Maupin, a small town on the Deschutes River, for two weeks because he felt that fly fishing together was just what they all needed. When chasing steelhead, other thoughts are flushed out, and the mind takes in the rhythms of moving water and the natural world. Six-packs, junk food, and the pursuit of the opposite sex would only distract the young men.

Rex checked his watch. "Time for bed," he said. "Up at 4:30 tomorrow!" Conversation dwindled, and each one headed for his room.

As Rex prepared for bed, he heard sounds outside—voices, car doors. He moved the curtains and peered through his window, searching for the source. The noises came from the house across the street. *I wonder who lives there?* he thought as he turned out his light. He closed his eyes and decided not to speculate about the neighbors. After all, it was nothing to do with him or the boys.

Day Two

AS AGREED, THEY AROSE AT 4:30. If any of them felt a lack of enthusiasm, he had the tact to hide it from Rex. Barry and Lonnie took the pickup and driftboat, planning to fish from Beavertail to Macks Canyon. Rex and Dwayne, his oldest son, took the other car and headed upstream from Maupin.

A steelhead grabbed Rex's fly on their second run, but the fish came unbuttoned after only a minute. He and Dwayne saw no other action that morning. They opted for lunch at the OK Cafe and were waiting for their burgers when Judd Boone, owner of the OK as well as the Rainbow Anglers Guide Service, stopped by their table. They chatted a bit about the steelhead season. After the usual pleasantries and fishing talk, Judd pushed his Stetson to the back of his head and asked if they were in town for a while.

"Two weeks," said Rex. "We—Dwayne, Barry his brother, and Lonnie my nephew—are staying at Evan Baxter's house."

"Nice place," Judd said. "Good river views. Evan had me over for dinner a couple of times. The place can handle a crowd—two bedrooms up, two down, shared bath on each floor. House across the street is big, too."

"I heard some people over there last night," Rex said.

"Probably Reina Jaeger. Excuse me, Reina *Francois*. Went back to her previous name after the divorce a couple of years ago. Reina kept the house in Maupin as part of the settlement. Likes fishing better than her ex. Always comes for two weeks at this time of year. Sometimes brings her kids. Two girls, Rose and Marie, maybe late twenties, unmarried. A son Kelly, a little older. Kelly's a veterinarian. Dogs and cats. Anyway, all of them enjoy fishing, but Reina likes it best. She's a fine fly caster."

A couple of single young women next door? This was not what Rex wanted to hear. The boys needed to work together, not individually or against each other. Barry and Lonnie were born two days apart and were more like twin brothers than cousins. They got along well but were fiercely competitive. He imagined a worst-case scenario: Barry and Lonnie fighting for the best-looking daughter, Dwayne being reminded every day of his recent divorce and how much he missed his two little girls. Rex sighed inwardly; you never stop worrying about your children.

But there was more. Every time the boys chased girls it recalled the happy days when he'd courted Sonia, his late wife. Rex was now in his late fifties—fit and trim and certainly young enough to rekindle love. Many of his friends were telling him he needed to "get out there." But how could he ever find anyone like Sonia again? Yes, he was lonely. But dating? The quest for someone new to share his life— the possibility of making the wrong choice—scared the hell out of him. He had friends who'd deluded themselves into disastrous second marriages. Deep down, he knew that The Pledge was more about him than the boys.

REX AND DWAYNE LEFT THE OK and fished the rest of the day, returning to the house around 7:00. Lonnie and Barry were already there. Lonnie was triumphant, having caught two steelhead to Barry's one. "That last one jumped six times!" Lonnie said, casting his voice in Barry's direction.

"Where are my binoculars?" said Barry, paying Lonnie no attention whatsoever. He rummaged in his tackle bag. "Eureka!" he said, and put the binoculars to his eyes. "Two SUVs ... four people ... a woman about Dad's age ... a thirty-something guy ... and two ... turn around! ... ah! Two young ladies, late twenties!"

"Dude!" Dwayne said. "They can see you in here looking at them. Try to have some couth."

Barry turned out the light so he'd be in the dark and resumed his surveillance. Lonnie elbowed him and grabbed for the binoculars. Barry turned so Lonnie couldn't have them. "Whoa," Barry said, "that one's really cute!" Lonnie moved to the other side, trying again for the binoculars. Barry turned away again. "The other one's pretty hot, too!"

He handed the binoculars to Lonnie. "You're right!" Lonnie said after a look.

"Boys!" Rex said, almost shouting. "You're worse than two tomcats sniffing around an alley. Put those binoculars down! You took a pledge."

"Oh, right," Barry said. "The Pledge. Mustn't forget ... *The Pledge.*"

"The Pledge doesn't say we can't look," said Lonnie. Even so, he put the binoculars on the dining table.

Rex sighed. They were young men, after all. "Well don't be so damned obvious about it. Dwayne's right—have some manners."

Day Three

THE NEXT DAY YIELDED ONLY one fish between the four of them, so they were subdued when they gathered at the house after sunset. Dinner was almost ready when Rex heard a knock on the front door. "It's them!" Lonnie said, rushing to the door.

Barry beat him to it, and Rex heard a creak of hinges followed by Barry's honey-voiced, "Well, hello."

Rex pushed in front of the two boys and saw a pretty young woman in a red wool shirt under the porch light. "Hi," he said. "Can I help you?"

She put out a hand. "I'm Rose, Rose Francois. Do you know anything about plumbing? I … my family … we're across the street." She turned and pointed. "We have a leaky pipe that's squirting water, and we don't know what to do about it."

"Glad to help!" Barry said. "I'll be right over."

"No hurry," said the young woman. "We've got some buckets to catch the water. At least for now."

"Well," Rex said, "dinner's almost ready, so *I'll* come over in half an hour, if that's okay." He turned and scowled at Barry, then faced Rose Francois. "In the meantime, you might turn off the main water valve. Do you know where it's located?"

"Mom might know," Rose said. "We'll try that. Thanks!"

After Rex closed the door behind her, Barry said sweetly, "I'll take care of it. After all, you always taught us that we should help people in need."

"How are you going to help them?" Rex said. "You don't know anything about plumbing!"

"Neither do you," Barry said.

"I'm good with plumbing," Lonnie said. "I'll go."

"I'll come with you," Rex said. "To keep an eye on you!"

Half an hour later Rose met them at the door of the Francois house. She introduced her brother Kelly, sister Marie, and mother Reina. They were an attractive family, Rex admitted. And it was clear where they got their good looks: the mother, Reina, was a tall woman in her mid-fifties with well-coiffed silver hair and a confident manner. She dressed casually but well. Probably a well-paid professional, Rex figured.

While Lonnie worked on the leaky pipe joint—and Rose and Marie stood by handing him tools—Rex chatted with Reina. She was plain-spoken, which Rex appreciated; he didn't like it when people wouldn't say what was on their mind. "Are you in business of some kind?" he asked at one point.

Reina nodded. "I'm a marketing manager for Intel in Hillsboro. What do you do?"

"Lawyer, sole-practitioner. Mostly small business clients. And personal issues for them—estate planning and the like. My office is in Lake Oswego. Evan Baxter is a client." He waved in the direction of the house. "He rented his place to me for two weeks."

"Two weeks?" Reina said. Her gaze wandered around the room to her children. "Starting when?"

"Two days ago."

"Ah. Lines up with our two weeks on the river." A cloud passed over her face. "Yeah. Well."

AN HOUR AFTER REX AND Lonnie returned to their house, there was a knock on the door. It was Rose and Marie. Each carried a plate of fresh cookies. "We just wanted to say thank-you," Rose said. "We really appreciated you coming to our rescue."

"Rose's cookies are chocolate chip," said Marie. "Mine are oatmeal raisin." They stood in the doorway, smiling and eager. Reina and Kelly hung behind, looking left and right at nothing in particular; neither seemed as pleased to be there as Rose and Marie.

Barry came quickly to the door and eyed the two plates. "Mmmm!" he said, "Chocolate chip! My favorite!"

Rex wanted to grab the plates and say thank-you-good-night, but the two young women obviously didn't want to just run a cookie delivery service; Rex invited them in.

For the next hour, Rose, Marie, Lonnie, and Barry filled the room with words. Kelly and Dwayne held a polite side conversation. Rex had little to say; Reina was the same. Rex caught her eye at one point—she seemed as wary of this turn of events as he did.

Day Four

THE NEXT DAY, REX PLANNED to fish with Lonnie, but Lonnie had other ideas. "You and Dwayne take the driftboat," Lonnie said. "Barry and I wanted to try some of the runs from the access road below Sherars Falls."

"Okay," said Rex. "I think we'll fish upstream. Put in at Nena, then fish our way back."

When Rex and Dwayne drove above town, however, they found several boats already on the water, so they changed plans and launched at Beavertail, below Sherars Falls.

Late that afternoon they saw the other two boys, and it was not a scene that pleased Rex. He'd anchored at Ferry Canyon, a very long run. After working through the upper sections, they walked downstream. The Pipeline run was across from them on the other side of the river. Barry and Lonnie were there, apparently giving spey casting lessons to Rose and Marie.

Rex clenched his jaw, and his face grew warm with anger. He put his fingers in his mouth and gave a loud whistle. Barry and Lonnie looked up, surprised to see Rex.

"Busted," Dwayne said quietly.

THAT NIGHT, REX TORE INTO Barry and Lonnie. "What's with you two? Huh? This was supposed to be two weeks of working together. A common purpose. The pursuit of steelhead. Instead, you two are chasing after every young lady that comes along."

"Hold on, Dad," Barry said. "We're not exactly chasing 'every young lady.'"

"Alright. Two young ladies. Mostly one, from what I can see. Still—"

"And we're not *chasing* them!" Lonnie broke in. "Remember— last night they came to us. And today we just happened to run into them at the Pipeline."

"We were *helping* them!" Barry said. "Last night and today. What were we supposed to do? Drive on by? Pretend we'd never seen them before? Say, 'Hi-nice-to-see-you. Sorry-we-can't-talk-we-took-The-Pledge.'"

Rex had plenty more to say, but there was a knock. When he opened the door, the mother—Reina Francois—stood under the porch light. "We need to talk," she said firmly. "Privately."

They moved away from the house and stood in the moonlight on the street. "I'll speak frankly," Reina said. "I'd like your sons to stay away from Rose and Marie. We came here for a family vacation, not a goddam mating dance."

"Us too," Rex said. "But let me be clear: Barry—the one with the thick beard—is my son. The blond one—Lonnie—is my nephew.

My older son, Dwayne, isn't involved." Somehow this distinction seemed important to Rex, although he wasn't sure why.

"Whatever, whomever. They're hanging around Rose and Marie like a couple of horny tomcats."

"Wait a minute," Rex said angrily. "It was Rose who came over asking for help with the plumbing. And your daughters who brought cookies and invited themselves into our house. So who's hanging around whom?"

"Did you just call my girls a couple of sluts?"

"Did you call my boys horny tomcats?"

They stood eyeball to eyeball for half a minute; then Rex said, "Well, they can act like a pair of tomcats, I know. But they're decent men, and honorable."

Reina's jaw worked a bit; then she said, "I admit that Rose can be flirty. She likes boys. Always has. I just don't want her to get hurt by someone who's only interested in one thing."

That set Rex off again. "Oh, excuse me," he said. "I didn't realize she couldn't think for herself and was underage. What is she? Fourteen? Fifteen?"

"Don't get lawyerly with me! Just tell your boys to stay away from my girls!"

"Works two ways!"

"Okay!"

"Okay!"

BACK IN THE HOUSE, REX FELT energized and loose, not tight and angry. Still, he put on a stern face and announced a new plan. "From now on," he said, "Barry and I are fishing together. Dwayne, you fish with Lonnie."

"What are we?" Barry said. "Ten years old?"

"You are but a tender junior," Rex said in a tone both ironic and authoritative.

"And you're a tough senior." Barry replied.

"Just do it!"

WITH THE MORNING LIGHT, however, things looked different. Rex was outside stowing lunch in the driftboat when Dwayne approached him; Barry and Lonnie were inside.

"Dad?" Dwayne said. "I think you need to back off a bit."

"Are Barry and Lonnie mad at me?" Rex asked. "Am I treating them like irresponsible teenagers?"

"Yes, they're a little upset. And yes, you're treating them like children."

Rex hunched a shoulder. He had a pain in his back, near the left shoulder blade. "Maybe you're right. Maybe I should back off a bit." He worked his left shoulder again.

"That shoulder giving you trouble?"

"I'm not used to so much fly fishing. Casting gets to me sometimes." He knew it was a partial lie; the stress of dealing with Barry and Lonnie was probably a bigger factor.

"Know what I'd do?"

About what? Rex thought. *A sore shoulder or Barry and Lonnie?*

"I use a lacrosse ball. I carry one with me just for times like this."

Rex still wasn't sure if they were talking about his shoulder or the boys.

"Put it on the wall between your shoulder blade and your spine. Then move up and down. It relaxes the muscles. A tennis ball isn't hard enough, but a lacrosse ball is perfect. I'll show you inside."

"I'll try it," Rex said.

"You also might want to back off a notch on Barry and Lonnie," Dwayne added.

REX KNEW DWAYNE WAS right. He had no enthusiasm for playing chaperone to adults. For the rest of the week, each man went his own way and made his own arrangements. Nonetheless, Rex tried to take the pulse of the situation by looking for subtle signs. But the dinner conversation was always about fishing, football, music, and movies. There were no more knocks on the door, no more plates of cookies, and no more shouting matches with Reina Francois. He wondered how she was doing.

The Second Week

AT THE START OF THEIR second week Rex fished alone, which suited him. The young men liked to fish hard all day, but he took a break and went to the house for an afternoon nap. Sometimes he used the lacrosse ball on his back; it worked well, and he was grateful for the tip from Dwayne.

One afternoon he came back to the house and saw Reina Francois in her yard. He felt bad that their last meeting had devolved into a shouting match, so he walked over to apologize. They had a pleasant conversation about the fishing. Rex found her to be a knowledgeable angler who knew the river well.

"One thing I miss," she said. "We don't have a driftboat, and I'd like to fish Don-and-Lola's." Don-and-Lola's was a well-known steelhead spot just upstream from Maupin. "I love that run."

"That's a good run," Rex said. "A classic." Then, without thinking, he said, "I have the boat this afternoon. I could take you there—" He suddenly stopped, thinking *What did I just say?*

Apparently Reina picked up on his hesitation. "Oh, don't bother," she said. "I shouldn't have mentioned it."

"No trouble. It's just ... " He sighed and told her about The Pledge.

"Well," said Reina, "I can see your dilemma." She looked away from Rex and added, "I got my girls to make a similar promise."

"Oh, let's just do it," Rex said. "We don't have to tell the kids."

REX LAUNCHED THE BOAT AND rowed them to Don-and-Lola's. "Why don't you take the upper half," he said to Reina, "and I'll fish the lower."

"You're being too generous. You rowed—you take the upper section."

Rex smiled and shook his head, then walked downstream.

Twenty minutes into his half, Rex heard a whoop. He looked upstream and saw a bright steelhead leap from the river; Reina had hooked a good fish. He waded upstream and helped her land a wild eight-pound steelhead. They released the fish and returned to their fishing. Near the end of his part of the run, Rex also hooked a steelhead. Reina came down and tailed a hatchery-raised buck for him, which Rex kept for the barbecue.

Reina stood near Rex while he cleaned the fish. "Good old Don-and-Lola's," she said. "It was great to fish it again! Thanks!"

"Yeah," Rex said. "Good run! At least for us!"

"It was my husband's favorite," Reina said. "Well, not Dan Jaeger's, my ex. Tony Francois'. The kids' dad." She paused. "He died six years ago. Cancer."

Rex nodded. He'd deduced her loss from her tone of voice. "I lost my wife three years back," Rex said. "Car accident." Each fell silent, a bond of grief between them.

After a couple of minutes, Reina said gently, "I'm sorry I lit into you the other night. About your boys. It's just that I worry about Rose and Marie. It's not like I'm guarding their virginity; they've been active since college. I know, they know, we each know the other knows. But we don't talk about it." She took a big breath. "They're grown-ups, but that's no protection from bad choices. Not that they've made any disastrous ones. But you worry. Kids can't always distinguish love from lust. Or understand how the two are connected. Or not. Love—if it comes from the wrong place—can be an evil angel."

Rex nodded; he appreciated this frank discussion. "Yeah, sometimes my boys seem to think sex exists solely for its entertainment value."

"Like cable TV."

Rex laughed. "But without as many channels!" He shook his head. "At least, I hope not!" He got serious. "I shouldn't talk about them that way. They talk worse than they act. And they're not ready to settle down yet. Well, Barry and Lonnie aren't. Dwayne is the only one who got married, and it didn't last."

"I understand. Rose and Marie play the field, too. Sometimes a little too casually for my taste." She spread her hands. "All you can do is tell them the basics—physical and emotional—and let them sort it out on their own. And hope for the best."

"As a parent," Rex said, nodding, "you have the perspective of time and experience. You know how easy it is to be distracted by the wrong things and make mistakes. But they don't want your advice! 'What could that old geezer possibly know about love?'"

"Ah yes! The young are always in love, and every month is May. And they think that for us—their parents—every month is January! They'll talk frankly about sex to everyone on the planet except us."

"Why is that?" he said. "What do they think? That I'm going to be shocked into speechlessness? That they'll utter the word 'sex' and I'll devolve into stammering? I can't talk to the boys about their love life." He turned away from her. "And they sure as hell don't want to hear about mine."

"You're their parent," Reina said drily. "You're not allowed to have genitalia or a libido."

"How do they think they got here?"

"I tell my kids I walked out of the nunnery one day, and there they were—floating down the river in little wicker baskets. It's the version they prefer."

"My boys like the stork story. Anything else is just disgusting to them."

Reina laughed. "I think sometimes they get an inkling that once we were young and just like them. But now we're old and … nonfunctional. Parents don't have thoughts … like that."

They were both silent again; then Reina raised her eyebrows. "Who am I to lecture them! I didn't just fall off the turnip truck, but that didn't stop me from marrying Jaeger The Jerk." She sighed. "What a piece of work he was. Anyway, thank god for lawyers and pre-nups!" She picked up her rod. "It's getting dark. Maybe we should get back across the river."

As they climbed into the boat, she said, "I've had my best talks with my son, Kelly. He's gay, and we had long, frank conversations about sexuality and relationships. By the way, it's okay with me. That he's gay. I hope you're not bothered."

"Me? No problem."

REX ROWED TO THE WAPINITIA boat ramp, where his pickup truck had been shuttled, and loaded the boat onto the trailer. As they were pulling onto the access road, Reina suddenly ducked below the dashboard. "Damn!" she said. "It's the Four Runner!"

Rex stopped his rig. A black Toyota SUV was coming down the road. Rex saw Marie at the wheel. She hadn't seen her mother with Rex—probably because she was too involved in conversation with her passenger, Lonnie, whose eyes were glued on Marie.

"Who was driving?" Reina asked from below the dashboard. "Rose or Marie?"

"Marie."

"Do you think she saw me?"

"Um, no."

"Good!"

"Yup. Sure."

As they neared the main road, Rex spotted Barry's car at the OK Cafe. He and Dwayne were going to fish together today, and they'd probably gone in for an end-of-day latte. Because it was dusk and the OK's lights were on, he could see the customers inside. He quick-scanned the room for Barry. He was in a booth. With Rose. Dwayne was nowhere.

Rex decided to say nothing to Reina, but she was too observant. "It's Rose!" she said, pointing at the OK. She'd have repeated her below-the-dash slouch but suddenly sat upright. "Oh my God! She's with Barry!"

"Uh, yeah. Barry. And there's something you should know about Marie and Lonnie."

ON THE WAY BACK TO THEIR respective cabins, Reina quizzed Rex about the boys. Were they really decent? Treat women with respect? Have jobs? Responsible with credit cards? Any ... you know ... health issues? Rex reassured her that Barry and Lonnie were fine. More than fine, really—at least for guys their age. Reina volunteered similar information about Rose and Marie.

They discussed whether they should do or say anything, but decided to keep their mouths shut. They'd check back in a couple of days and compare notes.

Day Twelve

TWO DAYS LATER, ON THEIR next-to-last day in Maupin, Rex fished alone. He had no idea where the boys were, and he didn't want to know. About noon, he grabbed a burger at the OK Cafe, then drove to the service station. One of his truck tires had a slow leak—it had taken a beating on the rough access roads—and he wanted it fixed. The station was busy, so he left the truck and walked to the house, figuring on a short afternoon nap.

He was barely in the door, however, when Reina Francois came over. He invited her into the house for coffee. "Any idea what's going on with our kids?" she asked while Rex poured.

Rex shook his head. "You?"

"Nothing." She took a sip of coffee, then asked about the fishing.

Rex was glad for the change of subject. They talked fishing and shared some stories from the river. When they paused, Reina began to rotate her right shoulder, grimacing. "I'm not used to spey casting for so many days," she said. "I get a little stiff."

"I know what you mean! You know what helps? A lacrosse ball."

"A lacrosse ball?"

"Yeah. Dwayne showed me. Hold it against the wall with your back, alongside the shoulder blade. Then move up and down." He demonstrated for her. "Try it!"

Reina did as he suggested. "Oooh! That does feel good!" She stopped and looked at the wall behind her. "I'm afraid it's leaving marks, though."

Rex examined the wall. "Hmmm. You might be right. I've been doing it in the same place, and there's a bit of a smudge there. I'd better clean it up before we leave."

Reina nodded. "Too bad. That was feeling pretty good." She paused. "Would you mind doing it for me? Just move it with your hand? It felt sooo good."

Rex hesitated. This seemed … personal. He should find a way out of doing it, but he couldn't think how. Besides, he wanted to do it. "Sure," he said, and pushed the ball up and down between her shoulder blade and her spine, getting both sides.

"Ahhh! That is so relaxing! But there's a tight spot next to my left shoulder blade. Would you mind getting it with your fingers?"

"Umm, okay," Rex said.

AN HOUR LATER, REINA pulled the covers up to her neck and smiled at Rex. They were in his upstairs bedroom. "I think we're going to miss the evening fishing," Reina said.

Rex ran a finger along her bare arm. He hadn't felt so relaxed since ... well, he didn't know when.

There was a noise downstairs. He stiffened; Reina was suddenly on alert too. "I think it's one of the boys," Rex whispered. "Lonnie was going to walk down the railroad tracks and hit some runs. Maybe he came back for some flies or drinking water." He heard a voice. "Yup, it's Lonnie. We'll just be quiet, and he'll go back to fishing."

There was another voice—not Lonnie's or Barry's.

"It's Marie!" Reina said softly.

Rex bit his lip. "That sneak! What about The Pledge?"

"Oh yes! The Pledge!" she said, lifting an eyebrow at Rex. "How dare they!"

"Maybe they're just getting a snack."

There was laughter from the living room, followed by two sets of footsteps coming up the stairs. Reina put a finger on her lips. They lay perfectly still. The footsteps went into Lonnie's room, and there was a click as the door closed.

There was more laughter and giggling from the room across the hall. Rex and Reina were perfectly still for ten minutes. The giggles were replaced with sighs. "I think I can get out now," Reina said. "Their focus is somewhere else." Reina silently rose from bed and slipped on her pants and turtleneck. She gathered her shoes, bra, and panties in her hand and opened the door. Rex stood behind in a pair of boxer shorts. Reina nodded at him, blew him a kiss, and tiptoed to the stairs.

The door to Lonnie's bedroom suddenly opened, and Marie appeared wearing only a shirt of Lonnie's draped over her shoulders. "Mom!" she gasped, pulling the shirt tight around her. Her eyes grew wide when she saw the contents of Reina's right hand. "Mother!" she said, shocked.

Lonnie appeared in the door behind her, wearing even fewer clothes. At the sight of Rex, he got as far as "Uncle ..." then pulled Marie back inside the room and shut the door. "Mother!" Marie said again, sounding more accusing than shocked.

Reina looked at Rex.

Rex nodded. He led her downstairs, making no attempt to be quiet.

As they neared the door, Rex heard the creak of footsteps on the deck. Barry appeared, followed by Rose. They were talking and unaware of Rex and Reina.

"Hello, Barry," Rex said as the pair came through the door.

"Dad!" Barry said.

"You remember Reina, Rose's mother."

Barry, mouth agape, nodded robotically.

"Mom!" Rose said. She looked at Rex in his boxer shorts, then saw Reina's right hand; a bra strap dangled beneath her fingers. "Moth-errr!"

"Hello, Rose," Reina said evenly. "Welcome to the real world."

"Dinner's at eight o'clock," Rex said. "At the Imperial."

"But ... but ..."

"Us and ..." he waved a hand at the house next door, "and them. All eight of us. Don't be late. Oh, and Lonnie's upstairs."

"With Marie," Reina said to Rose.

"See you at eight," Rex said.

Day Thirteen

THE NEXT MORNING BARRY and Rose went fishing together. Lonnie and Marie took the driftboat for a short float from Nena to Harpham Flat. Rex met Reina for breakfast. They chatted about their careers and their kids. Reina wondered where her son Kelly was fishing. "He's been real quiet this week," she said. Rex and Reina made plans to see each other for dinner next week back in the city.

By four in the afternoon Barry and Lonnie had headed back to town. Likewise, the Francois clan was gone. Two houses that had been so busy and active were now quiet.

Dwayne stayed behind to help Rex with the final cleaning and packing. While emptying the refrigerator, Rex said, "So much for The Pledge. It seemed like a good idea at the time."

Dwayne shrugged. "Just because things didn't go the way you planned, it doesn't mean they worked out wrong."

"I hope Lonnie doesn't feel he's settling for second best. He was interested in Rose, you know."

Dwayne shook his head. "Never. He always had eyes for Marie. Lonnie wanted Barry to *think* he was after Rose. If Lonnie had showed his interest in Marie, Barry might have gone for her instead. You know how competitive they can be."

"So Lonnie faked interest in Rose until Barry was committed?"

"Yes. And ignoring Marie made her more interested in Lonnie."

Rex paused before expressing a thought that had been nagging him. "I'm sorry you didn't find anyone in all this. You're the only one who stuck to The Pledge and the only one who was left out."

Dwayne took a deep breath before answering. "Dad, don't worry about me."

"I can't help but worry about you. Lonnie found Marie, Barry has Rose. Even your old dad stumbled into a new love interest. God knows where—"

"Dad, I did find someone these last two weeks. We've hit it off really well. While Barry and Lonnie were sneaking around after Rose and Marie, I was free to fish with someone I was attracted to."

"What? Who?"

"Kelly."

"Kelly who?"

Dwayne pointed to the house next door.

"But ..."

"I'm seeing Kelly. The veterinarian. Rose's and Marie's brother. Reina's ... gay son."

Rex struggled to digest this. Finally he said, "You were married for seven years! You have two children!" His breath was coming short. "Are you saying you don't like girls?"

"Yes, sometimes. But I also like men. Didn't you always wonder about me a little? Barry certainly did."

"Well ... yes. But you got married and had children, so I figured I was wrong, and ... You're gay?"

"No, Dad. I'm bi-sexual."

"Buh ... buh ... bi—? Really?"

"Yes."

"Are you sure?"

"Um, yes, Dad, I'm quite sure. And have been for many years. Are you upset?"

"Just ... just trying to understand it all. Trying to get used to the idea."

"Dad, think of sexuality as a spectrum from one to seven. One is totally opposite-sex-oriented, and seven is totally same-sex-oriented. Four is equal enthusiasm either direction. Most people are a 'one.' I'm more like a 'five.' Maybe a 'five-point-five.' I can get interested in women, but mostly I lean toward men."

Rex exhaled deeply. "Wow. Hmmm. Whoa."

"I know, it's hard. Took me a while to get used to it, too. Are you disgusted with me?"

"Never. Just adjusting. Trying to grasp it all."

"Do you think Mom would have been upset?"

Rex thought about this, then said, "Your mother loved you unconditionally. She always wanted you boys to be who you were and not to wear a mask. No, she would not have been upset." He paused, gathering his scattered thoughts. "And I'm not either. I'm glad you were honest with me."

Dwayne nodded, then said, "Dad, I want you to know that I was always faithful to Laura. I might be bi-sexual, but I'm monogamous."

Rex was slowly composing himself. After a few more deep breaths he said, "Was this a factor in your divorce?"

"Yes. I loved Laura, in my way. But there was a ... a lack of consistent passion and enthusiasm on my side. Laura and I talked about it for the last year. With her help I came to a better understanding of myself. So we split up and agreed not to discuss it with anyone until I feel the time is right. Now's the time. Sorry to spring it on you like this."

"Well, you're thirty-one years old. You know your own mind, and you don't need any lectures or advice from your old man. I'll say this though: I'm glad we're in twenty-first century America and not some other place or time."

Dwayne nodded.

"But," Rex said with a smile, "I take back what I said about you being the only one to keep The Pledge."

"I didn't break a single word."

Rex thought about The Pledge. "No late nights," he said. "No drinking, no overeating or junk food, no ... ahh. I see." He nodded. "You're right. You didn't chase any women."

"You'd probably feel better if I had."

Rex shook his head. "I feel better when you tell me the truth—even if I have to adjust my thinking."

"Thanks. And Dad? I'm sorry The Pledge didn't work out the way you wanted."

"Serves me right. It's tough to get young blood to obey an old decree."

"Better to find love than fish," Dwayne said. "Sometimes we have to lose our oaths to find ourselves."

Wasco

WHEN ASKED WHAT HE DID for a living, Ty Decker always answered—proudly and without hesitation—"I'm a rancher."

What he meant by *rancher,* however, was complicated. The word's meaning had shifted since his great-great-grandfather pulled together forty square miles on the high desert outside Maupin. Back then, *ranch* meant cattle and the cowboys who managed them. A generation later, the Deckers raised wheat as well as cattle. In his grandfather's time—The Depression—most of the land was lost to debt and foreclosure. They managed to keep half a section, a mere 320 acres, but it was productive land.

That was enough to support a few dozen head of cattle, a bit of wheat, a hayfield, and a Community Supported Agriculture garden in the greenhouse. Ty also did freelance auto repair—schedule permitting—and sometimes he rented out an old house that sat on the property. His wife, Florence, worked half-time at the Maupin school; being good with numbers, she also did part-time bookkeeping and tax returns for local businesses.

They lived frugally, so their various jobs allowed them to educate their son and daughter at community colleges and state universities. One was now a high school science teacher in Eugene; the other was a nurse in Pendleton. Neither child had any interest in keeping the ranch, and their parents agreed that was smart of them.

So to Ty, *rancher* encompassed a rich past, an uncertain future, and a present in which he did whatever was necessary to continue working his own land.

But lately something nagged at him: how could he call himself a rancher when he no longer owned a horse?

His last ride, an aged Appaloosa named Suzy Q, died over the winter. He knew that there was no practical use for a horse on his puny acreage; but he came from a long line of expert horsemen, and the Decker ranch had never before been horseless. He longed for a new ride—perhaps a horse like Quicksilver, a famous cowpony of his great-grandfather's day. Among his other talents, Quicksilver was reputed as the best cutting horse in the county, maybe in all of Oregon.

A painting of Quicksilver hung in Ty's living room over the fireplace. He could see it from the kitchen, and in fact he was looking at it this morning as he sat at the kitchen table, elbows resting on the worn Formica, sipping his second cup of coffee. His mind was busy sorting out the tools he'd need for the day's work.

"What?" he said. His wife, Florence, had just spoken.

"I said, Why don't you go look at that horse the Kelly girls are selling."

Ty stared into his coffee mug. "We don't *need* a new horse," he said after a pause.

"Maybe you do," Florence said gently.

TY HAD ABOUT A HUNDRED AND one chores on his list. On a
normal day he'd get ten of them done, but eleven things would go
wrong, leaving him a hundred and two jobs for tomorrow—none of
which required a horse. Still, he was curious, and it doesn't cost
anything to look. He sped through his ten chores for the day, and even
did a couple of extra ones, before he allowed himself the luxury of
calling on the Kelly girls.

The Kelly girls were neither named Kelly nor were they girls.
They were twin sisters, and their maiden name was Kelly, but both
were now widows in their late sixties. They'd moved back to their
family's old homestead—still called the Kelly place, even though
nobody named Kelly lived there anymore.

Like everyone around Maupin, Ty figured the Kelly girls would
live forever because the Lord didn't want them in heaven, and the
devil doesn't like competition. They weren't actually diabolical, just
tough. They'd had no brothers, and in their youth they'd helped their
father around the ranch, doing as much work as a man. Back then,
both sisters could ride like Comanches and did barrel racing on the
county rodeo circuit until their mid-thirties. Ty's rodeo career
overlapped briefly with theirs.

In the ancient con game called *horse trading,* Ty's motto was,
Harmless as a dove, wise as a serpent. He always told the truth—no
matter how bad it was—when selling a horse, but he never believed a
word anyone told him when he was buying one. However, he made an
exception for the Kelly girls because he had known them all his life.
What they would tell him would be the truth. It just wouldn't be all of
it.

"We bought him from a Montana cowboy that came through
here two months ago," said Mary Flannigan Kelly Kowalski as they
walked to the corral. "He's a cousin of Steve Schultz. Said he needed
to sell the horse so he could get a real job and get married."

Ty nodded. "How come your arm's in a sling?" he asked. "Must
slow down your right hook."

"Fell down," Mary said, not looking at Ty.

Her sister, Kathryn Flannigan Kelly Vechione, opened the corral gate for them. "He's a gelding," she said. "A chestnut, about 16 hands. We call him Wasco."

"Is he registered?" Ty asked. By this he meant, was Wasco from a breed, such as Appaloosa or Arabian? And did he have papers showing his lineage?

"No. The Montana guy got him as a yearling from one of those mustang lots."

Ty shook his head. "Those wild horses can be difficult," he said. "Some of them don't take easily to domestication."

"They can also be damn smart. And wait until you see him. He's not your typical mustang. There's a lot of Quarter Horse there. I suspect some rancher's stallion got loose and had a little peccadillo with a local wild herd, if you know what I mean."

They entered the corral, and Ty had his first good view of Wasco. He was athletic looking—well-muscled but not bulky. His eyes were intelligent and kindly and his manner calm.

Ty moved in slowly, circling the horse from five feet out, eyeing him from all angles and giving Wasco a chance to get used to his presence. He then moved closer and gently rested a hand on Wasco's neck. The horse's skin twitched slightly at first touch, then settled down.

"He's very steady," Mary said.

Ty said nothing, nor did he make any sign of agreement. He liked what he saw, but he maintained an appearance of bored disappointment while the Kelly girls spewed praise for Wasco.

"You want us to halter him?" Katie asked.

"I guess," Ty said.

Katie slipped on a halter and held the lead rope while Ty squatted beside Wasco's left front leg. He gently felt the leg, starting at the hoof and working his way up. Then he picked up the hoof and examined it. He repeated the process for the other three legs. After a few more minutes of feeling, squeezing, and lifting, Ty checked the horse's teeth, trying to determine his age.

"Why don't you trot him out," Ty asked Katie. She did, and Ty watched with admiration as Wasco moved with smooth assertion, like a wave in the sea. His legs were straight, his gait steady. Then Katie hooked a lunge line to his halter and cantered him on both leads. Again, steady and smooth.

"How come you're selling him?" Ty asked.

"We just didn't think he was a *lady's* horse," Katie said.

"Shoot, I didn't know you were ladies!" Ty said with a grin. The sisters didn't smile at Ty's little joke. But neither of them tried to kick him, so he figured they took it as a compliment. He had found out what he wanted: probably Wasco had bucked and thrown Mary, and that was how she'd injured her arm. It neither surprised nor bothered him that Wasco bucked Mary off. Ty knew that the Kelly girls were domineering and heavy-handed with horses—"if it's not doing what you want, hit it" seemed to be their motto. No doubt Wasco objected, as would most intelligent and spirited horses.

Ty looked at the ground and shook his head. "I don't know," he said. He poked at a fence post with his boot toe.

"He's got cow sense," Mary said. "That Montana guy used him for ranch work. Even did cutting. Said he was good at it."

Ty shrugged. "People say lots of things when they're selling a horse."

"Look at those eyes," said Katie. "You can tell he's smart from the quiet way he looks at everything."

The three of them went on for half an hour, Ty hedging while the Kelly girls extolled Wasco's virtues like he was the Second Coming. Finally, Mary said, "You want this horse or not? I can always call Hal Degner."

Ty took off his hat and scratched his head. "Kind of a lot of money."

"We can discuss the money part," Mary said, "now that you've decided you want him."

Ty got the cash down to half the asking price, but he agreed to fix a sagging gate, install new shocks on their old Dodge pickup, and lease their hay field at a price that would have raised eyebrows at the Rainbow Tavern.

Ty went home for his stock trailer, then returned to collect Wasco. Before he drove off, he frowned and shook his head. "I hope I don't live to regret this," he said. "You ladies drive a hard bargain."

"Well, like you said," Mary snorted, "we ain't ladies."

TY WAS MORE ENTHUSIASTIC about Wasco than he would let on to the Kelly girls. The next day he was up at first light, skipped his second cup of coffee, and went straight to Wasco. He led him around the corral and did ground work so the horse could get used to him, then rode for ten minutes, mostly walking with just a little trotting. He repeated this all week, lengthening the riding time until he was up to an hour and was cantering on both leads. After another week, Ty barely had to cue Wasco to get him to turn, halt, or change gaits.

Although he'd never say it out loud, Ty knew that Wasco was grateful to be with an expert rider who understood him and treated him well. They quickly built a foundation of mutual trust and respect. By the end of the month, Ty felt like he only had to *think* what he wanted, and Wasco would do it.

ONE DAY TY RODE WASCO TO a little knot of cattle to see how he would react. As advertised, Wasco had cow sense—an elusive quality that a few horses possess but most do not. A horse with cow sense instinctively knows what cattle are going to do and will boss them around the way a herding dog works sheep. So Ty decided on the ultimate test: he'd try Wasco as a cutting horse.

A cutting horse combines cow sense with athleticism. In the old days, cowboys used them when it was time for branding and—to put it in polite terms—converting young bulls into young steers. A rider would separate a single animal, which is tricky because cattle want to be with their herd and don't like going solo, especially when they can see that some indignity is about to occur. The horse would then block every turn, dodge, and feint, until the target animal gave up. Then other cowboys would bring it to earth and do the necessary tasks with a hot iron and a sharp knife.

In today's world, cutting horses still had a place, but it was in high-stakes competitions that were the domain of the rich and famous, not people like Ty Decker. Still, Ty wanted to give it a try.

He began by harrowing the large corral beside the barn. Then he saddled Wasco and drove a half dozen yearlings into the corral. The cattle bunched together at one end with their heads down low, giving Ty and Wasco a wary eye.

Ty reined Wasco cautiously into the herd and split them apart, with one bunch next to the fence and the other in the middle of the corral. Then he moved around the edge of the middle bunch and let them spill back into the main herd until only one was left. The lone heifer looked at her departing herd-mates and ran to catch up. Ty cued Wasco to cut her off. The heifer spun the other way to get around the rider and horse. Ty wheeled Wasco in front of the heifer. Ty used Wasco to block each move, but Wasco was not quite ahead of the heifer.

"Let's try again," Ty said to Wasco, "and I'll let you do this one." He separated a steer, then rested his rein hand on Wasco's neck and wrapped his right hand around the saddle horn. The steer scooted right. Wasco surged forward and cut him off. The steer hesitated, eyed Wasco, then shot to the left. Again, Wasco spun and kept himself between the lone steer and the herd. A feint right, then a turn to the left, a quick reversal and a long run to the right. Wherever the steer wanted to go, Wasco blocked his escape. They worked three more heifers and steers before quitting, and Wasco was flawless on each one.

In that part of his soul that Ty reserved exclusively for himself, he saluted his great-grandfather's horse, Quicksilver: "Old horse, now I know what you were like," he said quietly.

A MONTH LATER, TY ANNOUNCED at breakfast, "Florence, do you know how much money they get in competitive cutting shows these days?" He pushed a flyer to her. "See this? Next week is the Northwest Cutting Horse Festival at the fairgrounds in Salem. Wasco could enter an amateur class for horses over seven years old."

"Next week? Don't you have hay to get in?" She looked closer at the flyer. "Entry fee of $750! Is that a misprint?"

"No. I called and checked. We'll earn the money back, Florence. Look, the $750 gets you into the preliminaries. If you're in the top 20 percent, you go to the finals and get $1,000, guaranteed. The winner gets $6,500. Wasco is so good, we can't lose."

Two weeks after that, Ty loaded Wasco into the stock trailer, ready to head to Salem for the competition. Florence handed him his hat as he got into the pickup truck. "Are you sure you know what to do?" she asked.

"I think so. I've watched a bunch of videos on the Internet."

Florence raised an eyebrow. "Ah, yes," she said. "The Internet. The source of all wisdom." She gathered herself thoughtfully, then said, "Ty ... why do you want to do this? I'm not saying it's a bad idea. I just want to know why."

Ty chewed his lip. "Maybe by the time I get back I'll have an answer."

IT WAS LATE THURSDAY afternoon when Ty and Wasco arrived at the Salem fairgrounds. Preliminary competitive rounds had been going on since Monday, but the first round for Ty's group of forty-some horses was scheduled for Friday morning. The top eight horses would compete in a Sunday night final.

Ty drove his fourteen-year-old Ford pickup and rusty stock trailer to the lot behind the barns. He pulled between two expensive horse trailers with custom paint jobs and built-in living quarters for the owners. Similar rigs were scattered throughout the parking lot. The casual display of wealth made Ty feel small and out of place. "Old horse," he said to Wasco, "I feel like a pair of overalls at a tuxedo convention."

Ty paid his entry fee and went back to the truck. He gave Wasco some hay and grain. The fairgrounds rented horse stalls, but Wasco was to stay in the trailer. After eating ham sandwiches from a brown bag, Ty rolled out a sleeping bag on the seat of the truck and turned in for the night.

EARLY THE NEXT MORNING, Ty eased himself out of the truck. His clothes were rumpled, his hair was tangled, and he needed a shave. He was bent and stiff from a cramped night in the truck.

The door opened on the trailer next to him. A slightly paunchy middle-aged man stepped out. He wore a fancy western shirt, a leather vest, and a silver belt buckle the size of a salad plate. His boots were classy snakeskin. Ty had a glimpse of the inside of the trailer's living quarters: custom cherry cabinets, tasteful fabrics on the dinette seats, a half-empty bottle of expensive whiskey sitting on the table.

When the man saw Ty, his jaw dropped. He rolled his eyes, shook his head, and walked on. *I guess I don't look too good*, Ty thought. He found a men's room and cleaned up as best he could, then got Wasco ready for the preliminary round.

HE RODE INTO THE WARM-UP ring to get the kinks out of his horse, as well as himself. The top competitors wore flashy outfits and expensive boots, like the man in the trailer next to Ty. Ty's shirt was new, but the rest of his clothes worked for a living.

The large indoor arena was split in half. One half was the warm-up ring that Ty was in, and the other had a large wooden stand for the announcer. Flanking the announcer were two canvas booths set eight feet off the ground; a judge sat in each. The judges were shielded from each other so they could independently evaluate each horse and rider. A row of bright yellow plants stood in front of the announcer's stand. "Wasco," Ty said quietly to his horse, "I don't think we're at the county rodeo."

Closed-circuit TV cameras caught the action so each round could be seen from the warm up ring and other parts of the fairgrounds. Ty had read the rules a dozen times, but he took a break from the circling warm-up riders to watch the competition on the TV monitor. He wanted to get a better feel for what he and Wasco were supposed to do.

When Ty's number came up, he was tight as new-strung barbed wire, but he loosened up as he and Wasco rode into the herd of wary cattle. They had two and a half minutes to show the judges what Wasco could do. Ty picked a fresh, quick-looking heifer that would make Wasco look good. They separated it carefully, so as not to spook the others, and got a clean cut from the herd. Ty slowly lowered the reins to Wasco's neck, wrapped his right hand around the horn, and they were off.

Once Wasco was cutting, Ty lost all thought of anything else. It was just the two of them against the heifer's instinct to return to the herd. They worked well, like they had at home, and after two minutes the heifer was tired and frustrated; she stopped, panting. Ty let her go. He was remotely aware of applause from the sparse, first-round crowd. The clock showed a half-minute left; he picked another heifer and worked her until the buzzer went off.

They left the arena to applause and cheers, and Ty waited nervously for the score to show up on the TV screen. One judge gave him 70 points out of 80; the other gave him 71, for a total of 141. It was the best score so far that day. Ty closed his eyes and breathed deep.

After cooling Wasco down and putting him in the trailer, Ty watched the rest of the first-round riders in his group. Only two had higher scores than Ty. He and Wasco had made it to the finals.

AFTER ANOTHER CRAMPED night in the truck, Ty decided to treat himself to a hot breakfast. He was carrying his scrambled eggs and bacon away from the barn's concession counter when he heard someone call, "Ty! Ty Decker!" He turned to face an old friend, Don McMillan.

"Are you the famous Ty Decker?" Don said. "The guy everyone's talking about?" Ty was completely puzzled, so Don explained that the pros were talking about an unknown horse ridden by a shabby cowboy from Maupin. "So I heard *Maupin*," Don said, "and I wondered if it was you. When I heard *shabby*—well, that removed all doubt!"

Don and Ty had been buddies thirty-some years ago when they both rodeoed around eastern Oregon and Washington. They'd lost touch a couple of decades back.

"Where are you staying?" Don asked.

"No place in particular," Ty said.

"Are you sleeping in your truck? Come on, Ty. That worked when we were twenty. But now's different. I'm staying in a hotel, but there's a small living quarters in my horse trailer. Stay there tonight."

Ty looked at his boots. He was never comfortable taking favors from other people, especially when he couldn't repay them. But he thought about his back and how he and Wasco might do better on Sunday after a good sleep. "I'd appreciate it, Don. Those Ford seats aren't as soft as they used to be."

Don laughed and put an arm on Ty's shoulder. "I've got some horses out here today; then I leave tomorrow about noon. Unfortunately I'll miss your ride in the finals. So let's have dinner tonight and talk about old times. Eat hearty, 'cause I'm buying."

Ty thought a minute and decided he could pay Don back later out of his prize money. "You're on," he said.

THAT NIGHT OVER DINNER, Ty and Don swapped old rodeo stories and caught up on the past. Don had sold his family ranch twelve years ago. "Some folks from California bought it," Don said. "They come up about two weeks a year to 'get away from it all.'" He took a long drink of coffee. "They had enough money to burn a wet mule. Bought my place with pocket change. I drove by a couple of years ago. The porch was decorated with painted wooden geese with little blue ribbons around their necks." Don twiddled his fingers in the air with mock daintiness.

Ty shook his head, wondering how his place would look after he and Florence were gone.

"But after settling the debts," Don said, "I had enough cash to set up a horse training business. Now I'm doing cutting horses. I'm sorry I didn't see your ride. You've got people talking. 'Who's that guy? You seen that horse before? How much did he pay for that animal?'"

"And now they know that I'm nobody from nowhere and that I just lucked into a good horse. Are you making a decent living out of this? Out of training horses for other people?"

"I do okay," Don said. "Most of the horse owners are big-shot lawyers, top execs in corporations, and such like. Or their wives. Some are movie stars. There's a lot of money in this sport."

"I see what you mean about the money," Ty said. "The guy next to me in the parking lot has mud flaps worth more than my whole rig."

"Yup," Don said. "I can believe it. These people have high-paying, stressful jobs. They do cutting for recreation. And they like to pretend they're cowboys."

The two men fell silent. Ty's elbow was on the table, his chin resting in his hand. He stared blankly into his coffee mug.

"Ty," Don said seriously, "why are you here? This doesn't seem like your kind of show."

"Florence asked me that when I was leaving. I … I'm not sure. The horse is good and … well, you know how it is."

"Sure. A cowboy likes to show off his horse."

Ty gave Don a grin. "What can I say?"

"But it's more than that, isn't it?" Don was still serious. "It's about the painting hanging over the mantel. And all that goes with it."

"About Quicksilver. And the past."

"About generations of horsemen named Decker."

"I suppose."

"And more than that. You and me—we were born in the wrong century. We know who we are. Ranchers. Cowboys. But the world doesn't have a place for us anymore. Oh, maybe some remote corners of the West, but not where we live. Or where you live anyway, since I don't have a ranch anymore. So we do the best we can and try not to think about it too much."

"I guess I thought cutting competitions might be a way of combining the old and the new."

"This isn't like Quicksilver's day," Don said. "Back then, there was a purpose to cutting. But here, there's no branding iron at the end of the ride. And no one gets their balls cut out." Don took a deep breath. "Ty, I'll be frank. I'm not sure you'd be happy in this world. It's too … not you. It's definitely not a place where you can re-create the past. We'll never see those days again."

"Maybe not. But I wanted to give it a try." Another sip of coffee. "You're here."

"It's a living. It's hard to be a rancher when you no longer own a ranch. Unlike you."

"How do you get along with this crowd?"

"It works because they think I'm colorful. And quaint."

"How about me? Am I colorful and quaint enough?"

"Hold still, and I'll check."

They both put on poker faces. Don cocked his head to one side and studied Ty carefully. Then he cocked his head the other way and scrutinized him again. "I don't know, Ty," he said after straightening up. "You're colorful enough. But ... I hate to say this ... you're lacking in the 'quaint' department."

"Damn!" said Ty, still poker faced.

They stared expressionless at each other, then simultaneously dissolved into laughter.

"BARLOW UP, KEATON ON-DECK, Decker two-away," said the announcer Sunday night. An athletic-looking woman on a big bay Quarter Horse rode out of the warm-up ring and over to the gate leading to the competition arena.

"Guess we should just go home," Ty heard a man say. "She always wins." Ty stopped and watched the Keaton woman dismount and check her saddle cinch. When her turn came she mounted up and rode in, her face a model of confidence and determination.

"Keaton up, Decker on-deck, Fox two-away," said the announcer. Ty watched the TV monitor to catch Keaton's ride. A fresh herd of cattle had been brought in and milled around the end of the arena. They stirred as Keaton rode in.

It was a good ride. The woman's long, blonde braid swung back and forth as she and her horse worked the cattle for their two-and-a-half minutes. They were good, Ty had to admit. The judges thought so, too, and gave them a total score of 145, the highest so far. Keaton rubbed her horse's neck when she heard the score, then leaned back and patted his haunches. As she left the arena, she gave an emphatic high-five to one of the turn-back riders.

"Decker up. Fox on-deck. Bernadini two-away."

Ty rode in, nervous but not as much as the first time. He glanced around the arena. The stands were filled with people. The competition was sponsored by the Shriners as a charity fundraiser; portly, post-middle-aged men in red fez hats contrasted with the younger, leaner crowd in western attire.

Ty turned to the cattle. They stood in a tight bunch at the end of the arena. One steer rested his head on the rump of another, then tried to mount him. A heifer on the outside edge looked suspiciously at Wasco and Ty, her ears wiggling. Wasco's ears were active, too, swiveling this way and that as he picked up the sounds of the crowd. Ty was conscious of the smell of dirt soaked with cattle urine.

He glanced at the turn-back riders to make sure they were in position, took a deep breath, and nodded to the judges to start his time.

He moved in slowly and made a deep cut of the herd, splitting them and turning half away from the wall and out to the middle. He had picked his animal and let the rest spill off like a bovine river as they returned to the security of the group. Then it was just one heifer, and Wasco blocking her escape. Ty curled his right hand around the saddle horn, then slowly lowered the reins to his horse's neck. Now it was up to Wasco.

The heifer looked past Wasco at her departing herd-mates. Wasco lowered his whole body, evenly balanced over his four legs. Ty could feel Wasco's muscles flex as he prepared for action. Wasco stretched his neck, head low, and flattened his ears. He was eye-ball to eye-ball with the heifer. No heat-seeking missile ever had a tighter lock on its target. The cow squirted left. Wasco's weight was already on his haunches, and he swung his front legs around to block her, then moved his back end over so he was balanced again. The heifer spun and ran to the right. Wasco whirled and sped ahead of her. A run to the left, but again Wasco turned and surged in front. The heifer dodged to the right, stopped, then ran right again.

They moved back and forth in a straight line. Wasco was low and poised, his hocks almost in the dirt. He pivoted off his powerful hindquarters and swung his front legs around, then adjusted so he was square and ready. He had never moved so well. The heifer tried to run out the other end of the arena, but the turn-back riders drove her back to the middle, charging in on their horses, crying, "Chi-chi-chi-chi! Chi-chi-chi-chi!" This gave the heifer new energy, just what Ty and Wasco needed.

Dodge right, feint left, feint left again, spin to the right and make a break. Each time, Wasco was there, working off the strength of his hindquarters, shifting his legs and his weight, always balanced, low, and flat. Dirt sprayed from under Wasco's hoofs with each move. His mane flew back and forth with every spin and surge, and Ty's chaps flopped in unison. They were synchronous power and intelligence, the perfect blend of horse and rider. In the deepest part of his soul, Ty felt the thrum of emotion that comes when you know you are at one with a thousand pounds of athletic, animated, intelligent horse.

Ty never moved the reins, never cued Wasco with his legs. He concentrated on the heifer, anticipating Wasco's moves so he would always have his weight in the right place. The crowd stamped their feet, shouted and clapped, cheering on the unknown horse and the plainly dressed cowboy. Every move brought whoops and applause. Ty and Wasco were everything that horse and rider should be, and the crowd knew it.

The heifer was worked out and standing still. Ty looked to the clock. Forty seconds left. He let her go and went for another. He picked a steer off the edge. Before he started, he had a one-second defocusing: an image of him and Don McMillan having dinner and talking. Then his mind was back on track and he started to work the steer. Twenty-five seconds were left on the clock.

They started well, as before. Then the steer tried a dash to the left. Ty knew which way he was going from his eyes. Wasco spun hard. To the right.

There was nothing Ty could do. He blew out of the stirrups and came off his horse. His left shoulder hit first, and he rolled a couple of times in the dirt. He stood up stiffly, his shirt a blotchy green from a cow pie. He was dimly aware of a prolonged, disappointed "Ohhh" from the crowd. The buzzer went off; his time was over.

"Ty, I think you zigged and your horse zagged," the announcer said like he had invented humor. Some of the crowd laughed. "Folks, how about a hand for the cowboy from Maupin?" There was applause, and the next rider came in.

Ty picked up the reins and left the arena. They would get a token score that would put them in last place.

THREE DAYS LATER TY WAS driving by the OK Cafe in Maupin. He saw Hank O'Leary's truck out front, so he parked and walked into the OK. He found Hank in a corner booth eating breakfast. "Hank," he said after sitting opposite, "you were raised on a ranch. Maybe you can help me puzzle out a horse problem."

"Ty, if you can't figure it out, I'm sure I can't. But I'll listen."

Ty described what had happened at the cutting horse show, finishing with, "I had the vet check him out when we got home. He couldn't find anything wrong."

"Sometimes these things aren't obvious. You wish your horse could talk and tell you where it hurts."

"Well, I tried to buy Mr. Ed," Ty said, "but he wasn't for sale." He rubbed his chin. "Do you think it's an attitude problem?"

"Perhaps. You know how opinionated horses can be."

"He dumped one of the Kelly girls before I bought him."

"That doesn't mean much," Hank said. "The way those girls treat horses ..." Hank took a bite of hash browns and chewed thoughtfully. "So you went left, and the horse went right. Maybe he's trying to tell you that cutting competitions aren't the right thing for you and him. Maybe your horse was delivering a message."

"He's a smart horse, but … I dunno."

"Still … you wanted to go one direction, and your horse thought it was the wrong way. Is that what they call irony?"

"No, irony is something else." This came from Logan McCrea, who sat ten feet away by the espresso machine. Logan lived in Ty's rental house; his nineteen-year-old daughter, Samantha—Sam—ran the OK's espresso machine. Logan often sat beside her when he wasn't out on the Deschutes working on his guidebook.

"Logan," Ty said, "you know horses, and you've seen Wasco. What do you think?"

"I think my daughter knows horses a lot better than I do." He looked at Sam. "Any ideas?"

Sam looked like she might have an opinion, but just shrugged.

"Go ahead," Ty said softly. "Tell us what you think."

"Das Pferd ist der Spiegel Deines Inneren."

The men looked at each other, puzzled. Logan said, "My German is pretty rusty, but … Pferd—horse; Spiegel—mirror; Inneren … I don't recall that word."

"The horse is the mirror of your innermost thoughts." Sam said. "That's what Eva, my dressage instructor, used to tell me. She's German. If you tense your left forearm, your horse will tense its left foreleg. Stiffen your back and your horse will stiffen its back." She cocked her head. "At least, if you've got a good horse and you're in tune with each other."

"So …" Ty said. "I … no … um … I have no idea what to do with that information."

"So, Sam, what you're saying is … " Logan looked at his daughter expectantly.

"Deep down," Sam said, "Ty knew competitive cutting wasn't right for him and his horse. He gave a conflicting signal, and Wasco went the wrong way. And ... " she paused and gathered her breath. "The cue may have been mostly mental—Ty's subconscious thoughts, his doubts that he was—"

"My doubts that I was going in the right direction. Doing the right thing." Ty said quietly.

"Did you have any doubts?" Logan asked.

Ty thought back to his conversation with Don McMillan, then recalled his flashback just before starting his second cut in the finals. "Yes," he said. "But I tried to shut them out. I think I knew I was going down the wrong road. I just didn't know I knew it."

"What did you know ... that you didn't know you knew?" Hank asked.

Ty took a deep breath. "That modern cutting horse shows are for rich people who want to pretend they're cowboys. But those shows aren't for actual cowboys—"

Logan shook his head. "Now *that's* irony."

"I think ..." Ty said, looking at his boots. "I think it really hit me ... finally sunk in ... that the old days are ..." He closed eyes and shook his head. "That everything me and my family worked so hard for ... for all those years ... that whole way of life ... is coming to ... I was trying to drag the past into the future. But the future doesn't have a place for ... I guess I knew that, but I didn't want to admit it. Because I knew how ... because I knew how bad it would make me feel."

"Sometimes," Hank said softly, "you have to go a few extra miles down the wrong road ... just to know *why* it's the wrong road."

ON A BRIGHT MID-OCTOBER morning, Ty loaded Wasco into the stock trailer and headed south on Highway 197. Not far from Shaniko Junction, he turned onto a one-lane gravel road that bisected a ranch owned by his friend Ron Bauer. The road was paralleled on both sides by barbed wire fences strung between metal T posts; additional stability came from occasional round cribs made of wire and filled with lava rock. Grass, sagebrush, and juniper dotted the thin rocky soil of the high desert behind the fences.

Ty parked his rig at a simple gate, leaving enough room for a vehicle to pass. He unloaded Wasco and led him through, then closed the gate behind them. He put his foot into the stirrup, lifted himself into the saddle, and rode down a faint trail.

The Bauers owned over 15,000 acres outright and leased another 9,600. Their property extended to the Deschutes River, but today Ty and his horse headed for a rugged promontory about six miles distant.

For the first mile, they moved at a steady walk so Wasco could warm up. After that, Ty varied the gaits from walk to jog to a ground-eating extended trot and occasional lope. Regardless of the gait, Wasco moved sure-footed over the uneven ground, helped by Ty's perfect balance in the saddle.

A little under an hour later, Ty and Wasco reached the summit and halted. Ty rested his arms on the saddle horn and took in the view. Wasco's ears were forward and alert, his head moving slowly back and forth, his breath rhythmic and steamy in the cool air.

Since the cutting competition, Ty had been riding Wasco to this place once or twice a week. At first he'd felt guilty about taking time for himself, time to be with his horse—*on* the land rather than *working* the land. But somehow the work got done anyway, so his conscience no longer nagged at him. These rides gave him perspective, and he'd realized that *perspective* was more important than any ranch job.

To the west, low hills rolled like waves to the Cascade Range. The morning sun highlighted each lift with golden hues and etched every valley in dark shadow. Above green foothills, the volcanic cones of the Cascades spread north and south across the horizon, a panorama limited only by the curvature of the earth; the tallest peaks glistened from fresh snow. Two thousand feet below Ty, the

Deschutes River twisted through its canyon, patiently turning solid rock into tiny bits of sand that would end their journey in the Pacific. Even at this distance, he could hear the roar of the river.

Ty took deep, slow breaths, then let his vision expand until he could see from horizon to horizon, until the mountains and canyons and river filled his mind like the crisp, sage-scented air filled his lungs and gave him life. He knew that this view existed thousands of years before any Deckers claimed a piece of the high desert as their own. And it would still be here after he and all the Deckers before him had faded from memory and all trace of their accomplishments and failures, dreams and disappointments were dust in the wind.

He took in the view until he felt his past, present, and future merge into a single timeless moment. Then he patted Wasco's neck, and they turned for home.